Love Interrupted

BY RENEILWE MALATJI

Catalyst Press
Livermore, California

Catalyst Press

Livermore, California

Love Interrupted

Copyright © Reneilwe Malatji, 2018 . All rights reserved.

No part of this book may be used or reproduced

in any manner whatsoever without written consent

from the publisher, except for brief quotations for reviews.

For further information,

write Catalyst Press, 2941 Kelly Street,

Livermore CA 94551

or email info@catalystpress.org.

Originally published by Modjaji Books (South Africa)

FIRST EDITION 10 9 8 7 6 5 4 3 2 1

Library of Congress Cataloguing-In-Publication Data 2018930033

Cover design by Karen Vermeulen, Cape Town, South Africa

For my son

Mohale Malatji

and my best friend

Barry Millsteed

TABLE OF CONTENTS

Angela

"It's a girl," said the gynecologist, smiling and lifting up the baby for the mother to see. The maternity nurse stepped back. Her overgrown, jelly-like tummy trembled with each step. She poked the other nurse with her latex-gloved hand, leaving a red blood mark on her green, apron-like uniform.

"Mh! Mh! Mh!" the nurse said, unable to hold it in.

Having exchanged questioning looks, their eyes rested on the child as if they were looking at an alien. It had been a normal delivery, with no complications, and both mother and child were healthy.

The doctor put the child on Mpho's chest, with the umbilical cord still connected to the mother. Mpho raised her head and attempted to embrace her new daughter.

"Eh!" she gasped. "This is not my baby!"

Mpho addressed the gynecologist, an elderly white man, who was now standing next to her husband. The gynecologist gave the nurses a sharp look and ignored Mpho's comment. He took some utensils out of the steel trolley and gave them to the nurses to hold.

"Doctor, this is not my baby," repeated Mpho, the veins standing out on her neck. She lifted the child so that she could see its face, looked into its eyes, and laid it back onto her chest. She looked away, focusing on the leaves of the marula tree outside the small hospital window.

The gynecologist took off his soiled gloves and moved to the foot of the bed, where Mpho's husband, Matome, stood motionless as an Egyptian mummy.

The doctor's green eyes looked straight into Mpho's brown ones. He was still holding the two gloves in one hand when he said, "But it came out of you." He looked at Matome and shook his grey head.

The two nurses stood still, their eyes rolling from baby to husband and then to the mother. Mpho's husband was sweating as if he were the one who had just given birth.

"Are you really the father?" one of the nurses asked impulsively.

Matome nodded, streams of sweat flowing down his face and neck. He fell to the ground in a faint. It was understandable. Most African men couldn't take the heat of the delivery room, which is why a lot of them didn't go in there when their wives were giving birth.

An hour later, Mpho's parents arrived at the Mediclinic in Polokwane. Matome had been resuscitated and was now sitting on a chair next to the bed. Mpho's mother, a bubbly, light-skinned woman in her late fifties, a retired nurse, went straight to the small transparent cot. She examined the baby with a grandmotherly fussiness, to check if it was healthy. Her eyes widened when she saw the baby's face. For a few seconds, she was speechless and motionless. She then called her husband, who was still standing next to the door, holding a bunch of pink carnations in one hand and a copy of *True Love* magazine in the other.

"Hlabirwa, come closer and look at this miracle," she said to her husband, calling him with his clan name. "This is my grandmother in person—she has come back to life. This child looks exactly like her, look at the forehead, the eyes. *Yaa neh*! These things do happen. This child has taken everything from my side of the family. Look at that straight English nose."

When no one responded, she said, "Matome, did Mpho ever tell you that my grandmother was colored? Her father was a real white man. That gene is back in the family. Yes nana," she said to the baby, "*wena ke wena yo mobotse*. You are beautiful. Here Matome, you hold her. God has blessed us. We are so happy.

She is an angel. Let papa hold you, my girl."

Mpho's mother placed the child onto Matome's lap. At that moment Mpho decided on a name: Angela. Holding the child seemed to intensify Matome's dark complexion. His smile was strained, and a minute later he gave the child back to its mother.

"You must feed her, she must be hungry," he said in a nervous tone.

The ward nurse stood there looking at them as if she were watching *Alien 3*.

"Nurse, you can go. We will call you if we need anything," said Mpho's mother, banging the door after her, as if she owned the hospital room.

From that day on, sharks and crocodiles lived inside Mpho, eating away at her stomach.

Everyone who came to see the baby couldn't help being astonished. The little girl was nicknamed Happy Sindani. This was the name of a young colored boy in Johannesburg who was in the media because of paternity issues. Happy claimed that a certain prominent white businessman, whom his mother had worked for as a domestic worker, was his biological father. The man denied the possibility of being the father, and the whole thing became a media frenzy.

Mpho avoided going out with the child because of people's reactions. Mpho and her husband were the model middle-class family, "black diamonds," as they were called in South Africa—the new middle class that mushroomed after the African National Congress took over the apartheid government. They were distinguished by their conspicuous displays of consumption: big houses, expensive cars, and gadgets like Apple Macs, iPads, and fancy cellphones. The birth of this child posed a threat to Mpho and Matome's standing.

Mpho tried to continue with her life as if everything were normal, but the sharks and crocodiles would not leave her alone. Some nights in her dreams she would see them biting at and pulling apart her baby girl.

When the child turned four months old, Mpho and her husband held a big baptism party. Even though they'd been reluctant to show off the baby, a lavish party was expected of them, and was an opportunity to flaunt their wealth.

All their relatives were there, including Mpho's aunt MmaPhuti. A traditional lunch with delicacies such as *mogodu* and *dikgwatla* were prepared for the guests. All kinds of alcoholic and non-alcoholic drinks were served, including Rakgadi MmaPhuti's ginger beer.

Aunt MmaPhuti was well known for what she called her killer cooldrink, and her big mouth. She had overfed and bloated opinions about everyone and everything in the family. Years of being a *shebeen* owner in Seshego township had given her insight into troubled souls. She knew exactly where it hurt in everyone, and had made a hobby out of reminding people of these soft spots.

Rakgadi MmaPhuti's *shebeen*, which was in her home, was strictly for the middle-aged, well-educated, and prosperous. Often you would find her chasing adolescents and other unwanted patrons away before they even got inside her gate. "What do you want? Who told you I am selling alcohol here? I don't. Go! Go! Go!" She would scream like a crazy person to scare away those she felt were not fit for her high-class establishment.

Her affection for the affluent was reciprocated. They loved drinking at her place. Most times you'd find them squashed into all corners of the small living room. They would be discussing important issues to do with education, politics, and current affairs. Knowing very little about these things did not keep MmaPhuti from joining in the clever conversations. She would throw in a comment or two in her almost incomprehensible but confident English. "Yes! Correct. Thabo Mbeki is a difficulty man," she would say, proud to have been able to contribute something.

At times, she was helpful in solving difficult and secret issues in the family. She helped people to face things that they were afraid to confront. But most of the time her interference was destructive before becoming helpful. People fought and spent years not talking to each other because of her disclosures. Nevertheless, most people in the family still confided in and enjoyed gossiping with her. There was a side of her that always drew people to her. You would never miss her in any family occasion. Invited or not, she would be there.

Everyone loved her ginger beer and would take their turn at the drum to have a glass or two. She always sat outside, in front of the kitchen, with a jug, calling everyone to come and have a taste. She would add a nip or two of whiskey into the drum at intervals, after which she'd declare that the party would never be boring.

She offered everyone a glass, especially those that she knew did not drink, as well as children. Then she would comment on how merrily the children were playing—crediting it to the ginger beer. Or saying, "Look at so and so —she says she doesn't like alcohol, but look at her! She came here five times for the ginger beer."

After taking a considerable number of sips herself, she would end up deserting the drum to mingle and reveal the family secrets. Yet she never drank enough to lose her excellent faculties.

Mpho was carrying dirty dishes into the kitchen when she bumped into MmaPhuti in the dining room.

"Oh! My favorite niece! Where have you been? I have been looking for you everywhere," said MmaPhuti.

"Rakgadi MmaPhuti, how are you? I have been looking for you too. But this time I am not drinking your ginger beer. You know I am still breastfeeding," said Mpho.

"Rubbish! That ginger beer is good for your child. It will make her intelligent."

"No, no, no!" said Mpho.

"You know nothing. Your mother drank a lot of it when she was breastfeeding you. See how you turned out: clever."

Mpho laughed and said, "I know you are joking. I can't drink alcohol when I'm breastfeeding."

MmaPhuti shook her head. "Anyway! I have been meaning to talk to you about that. Come, let's go to the bedroom."

"Rakgadi, you want to teach me how to breastfeed. This is my second child. Believe you me, I know how it's done."

MmaPhuti grabbed the dirty dishes from her hands and placed them on the side board. She took Mpho's hand and dragged her towards the bedroom. She staggered, leaning one hand against the wall. She smelt like a brewery. In the bedroom, she closed the door and asked Mpho to sit on the bed, where the child was sleeping soundly. She took the baby's white satin blanket off and said, "Haa! Tell me! Where did you get this child? Green marble eyes! This one's father is a white man, not even a colored. A *lekgowa*, or my name is not MmaPhuti. This child can't be Matome's, with that navy-blue complexion of his. No!"

She was then silent for a few seconds, examining the sleeping child. "Unless it is Jesus Christ's Second Coming," she added.

Mpho was caught off guard and did not know what to say.

"How did you find a *lekgowa*, my girl? You are so bold. Mhhh ... You can babysit a lion's litter."

"You are drunk. You should stop drinking. It makes you paranoid. Leave me and my child alone. You are jealous because your children are not married and now you think you can destroy my marriage," said Mpho, holding her baby, who was now awake and crying bitterly. "Get out! You bring in evil spirits to my baby. Get out!" Mpho pushed MmaPhuti out of the room with all her strength. She could feel the sharks and crocodiles begin to tear at her insides.

Two years later, Mpho's marriage ended. Reasons unrelated to the child were cited for the divorce. The air in their house had always been filled with thoughts and things that remained unsaid. Matome was the kind of man who refused or lacked the ability to see the dark side of people and things. He interpreted life in the simplest way, like a child.

The real romance between them died when Angela was born. They had become no more than a habit to each other. Loving her husband felt like routine to Mpho—in the same way that cleaning the house or doing the washing did. Incompatibility and irreconcilable differences were the grounds mentioned in court. When the maintenance claim was made, Mpho asked Matome to pay for only one child. Matome had never confronted her on the paternity of Angela. Even after the divorce, Matome did not contest anything.

It was not until after the divorce that Mpho's sister Linda casually confronted her about the child's paternity, over a bottle of chardonnay. They were both tipsy when Linda finally found the courage to bring up the subject.

"Mpho, I am worried that if you die today from an accident, and some white man comes here and claims to be Angela's dad, our father is going to finally get a chance to use his gun."

Mpho laughed. "All he's done since he bought it five years ago is polish it. I'm sure he won't think twice if he gets the opportunity to shoot. He will shoot to kill," she said.

Linda took advantage of the mood and asked, "Who is he and where can I find him?"

"Hee! You mean Schoeman?" said Mpho, talking between mouthfuls of wine. "I don't know. Maybe he is a hobo somewhere. I haven't seen him since I stopped working at the Modikwe mine. He's probably still working there."

"So he works at the mine? We must find him. He must support the child," said Linda.

This conversation paved the way for Dawie Schoeman and Mpho to meet again. Discussions between the two of them led to a paternity test, which confirmed Dawie as the father. Dawie was not as shocked as Mpho had expected him to be. All he wanted was to see the child.

A week later, they waited in a restaurant for Linda to bring Angela. Mpho thought it might be confusing for her other daughter, who was 8-years-old, if they met at her house. She felt like a heavy load was about to be lifted off her. She was tired of explaining to the world and its mistress why her daughter looked the way she did. Now things would be out in the open. Everyone would know that Dawie Schoeman was the father.

Just yesterday, when Angela had come home from crèche, she'd asked Mpho if she was white or black. A question Mpho had never expected and did not know how to answer. Fortunately, Linda quickly responded and told the child that she was both—a little bit white and a little bit black. The response seemed to satisfy the three-year-old girl.

"God has a sense of humor," Dawie said. "My wife and I have been trying to have a child for fifteen years. We've consulted every specialist in the country and we even tried in vitro many times, but none of that worked. I have prayed for a child every day and I thought God had turned a deaf ear or lost my address. Wow, and this is how he responds."

"Your ways are not his ways," said Mpho. She recalled the night, four years ago, when they had shared a meal over a bottle of red wine at the Ocean Basket. That was the night Angela was conceived. She wanted to remember it as a night of passion, but it hadn't been. It was a night of drunkenness that resulted in a love child. It happened after they had become close friends while working at Modikwe mine. Dawie was good company and Mpho enjoyed his ability to turn anything into a joke. He made her laugh at a time when things were not going well in her marriage.

The night they went to the Ocean Basket was not a planned thing—they never anticipated that it would end the way it did, with them in a hotel room. He was her boss and they were both very drunk. What she recalled was that there were no fireworks—in fact, it was a disaster. Up to this day she could never figure out what happened to the condom. On Dawie, the condom had seemed oversized, dangling from all sides. She still could not believe that a child, a life, had emanated from all that.

Now, waiting for her daughter to arrive, she asked him,

"Did you tell your parents that they have a granddaughter?"

"My parents are dead. They would not have accepted a colored granddaughter. Even now they must be turning and tossing in their graves."

"Oh, here they come," said Mpho as Linda and her daughter walked into the restaurant.

Dawie jumped up from his chair. He wanted to embrace the child but could not.

Mpho said, "Angela, come closer, this is your real father. Say hello."

Dawie reached out to shake her hand. The small girl looked at him for a few seconds and then turned away.

They moved to follow her, but when the girl looked back, she screamed at the top of her voice, "Mama, *ke a motshaba!*" I am afraid of him.

Even though Dawie did not understand Sepedi, he backed off.

The child stopped crying. "I want to go home," she said.

This was the closest she had ever been to a white man.

Drama Queens and Kings

"I am sorry, we're fully booked for the night," said the lady, who appeared to be the manageress, before we'd even reached the restaurant door. She stood there waiting, with a "There's no way you are coming in here" look on her face, one hand resting on the doorframe and the other on her waist. Insects were gathering around the lamp above her head.

"But madam, we've booked a table for nine. It was confirmed earlier today," said my brother Tebogo.

"I'm afraid we don't have any tables available," said the woman. She was dressed in black pants and a white shirt, and wore her nose on her forehead. Her pale, tetchy face was etched with contours, lines that became deeper as she talked. Her collarbones protruded sharply, like knife blades. She spoke in a loud voice, as if we were standing a kilometer away.

The autumn sun had vanished into the skies, and the coastal wind blew hard and cold on our ears. Although you could not see it, you could hear and feel the living sea close by.

"Someone confirmed our booking and gave us directions on the phone five minutes ago," said Tebogo.

"I told you, we're full. There is nothing I can do," she said. She removed her hand from the doorframe and stepped back into the restaurant, her body blocking the entrance. Clearly, she expected us to leave. We were shocked. We had not anticipated such rejection after the joyful day we'd had in Grahamstown, mingling with intellectuals during my graduation ceremony.

Earlier, when we arrived at the restaurant and got out of the Toyota Kombi that my brother had hired at the airport,

I thought I saw people peering at us from inside, but quickly dismissed the idea. The Kombi resembled one of those notorious township minibuses. Our cheerful chatting and laughter must have unintentionally announced our arrival. It had been a while since anyone had graduated in my family, and it was cause for celebration.

"Is this the only Link-up restaurant in Port Alfred?" Tebogo asked again.

"Yes!" she said.

"Maybe you could check your reservations again, because I am sure we have a table booked for nine people," said Tebogo, scrolling through his cellphone.

My 17-year-old son, Mohale, who was standing next to one of the restaurant's front windows, said: "Eh, *malome*, I see there is a table inside with nine chairs and a reserved sign on it."

Tebogo was now on the phone with his personal assistant, Anna-Marie. She was an efficient 62-year-old Afrikaans lady who had become more of a family member to all of us than an employee. She was the one who organized everything: the flights, the hotel, and restaurant bookings. She had phoned me earlier in the day to wish me a pleasant trip.

"Hello, boss, is everything OK?" said Anna-Marie.

"Anna-Marie, we are at Link-up restaurant and there is a very touchy lady here telling us we don't have a booking," said Tebogo.

"Impossible! That is nonsense. Give her your phone," said Anna-Marie.

We never got to hear the conversation between Anna-Marie and the skinny manageress, because she immediately took the phone and disappeared inside, leaving us standing at the door.

She returned a few minutes later with a smile befitting a toothpaste ad.

"Sorry, there has been a misunderstanding. Your table is ready. Follow me."

"I told you there was a table reserved," said my son.

We walked in, one by one. The manageress stood beside the door in the same way that air hostesses did when you boarded a flight. Her nose was now in its right place and she smiled at each of us as we passed, though no one smiled back.

"That's a lovely outfit," she said as I entered. "Very different." And when my mother came in, she complimented her lavender suit.

"Flattery will get you everywhere," my mother said, marching in without looking at the woman. We all burst into laughter.

According to Anna-Marie, this was one of the classiest restaurants in Port Alfred. I wondered why. The space was so closely packed that our chairs touched those of the tables next to ours. It looked like it had been a residential home which was converted into a business. The décor was plain, with dull, off-white walls.

Inside, we were something of a spectacle. All the other tables were occupied by white people, who twisted and turned from their seats just to get a glimpse of us. It was as if we were exotic creatures in a zoo.

By the time we were settled at the long table, it was 7:30 in the evening and already dark. Fifteen minutes passed before our waitress appeared. A young girl, who might have been in her early twenties, dumped a pile of menus on our table. My sister Kgaugelo distributed them to everyone. The menus were large and leather-bound, like books of old maps.

Another fifteen minutes passed and still we'd received no service. At one point the young girl who'd brought the menus said, while passing our table and without even looking at us, "I'll be with you soon, we are very busy today."

Now it was my brother's nose that was out of place. I learned later from his girlfriend, Maseapo, that he is normally not this tolerant in such situations.

"If we were in Johannesburg, there would have been a scene. He can be very theatrical, he is a drama king. He would normally have staged a ballet on the table top, I tell you. Maybe he just didn't want to spoil your day," said Maseapo.

Kgaugelo and Maseapo claimed that they preferred the Pan-Africanist approach in circumstances like these. As my eyes scanned the room, I discovered that the restaurant was not even full; there were about four empty tables.

"I think we are being punished for our past sins," I said.

"Or the sins of our ancestors," said Molatelo, a friend of mine who was also graduating.

"They'll serve us eventually. Let's just sit here and be darkies, like they think we are," said Kgaugelo.

"What? I don't think that's a good idea. What if they serve us at ten? I am diabetic, I can't wait that long. I've already taken my insulin shot," said my mother.

"No, Mma, don't worry. Let's behave like we are having a good time, be loud and make a noise, and they will all leave. Then we'll have the place to ourselves," said Maseapo.

"I don't want a scene on my sister's big day," said Tebogo.

"These are the English. They're not big on scenes. They were taught before they were born how to be polite. They are not like the Afrikaners. They would rather leave quietly, to make a statement," said Kgaugelo.

"Why don't we do the same?" I said.

"Yes! Let's go. They are treating us like lepers," my mother agreed.

"No! If you do that, you are giving them what they want," said Kgaugelo.

"It's no longer about them. We just want to have a peaceful, decent dinner. Maybe we should settle for the buffet at the Fish River hotel," said Tebogo, getting out his phone again. The hotel was about twenty kilometers away, along the coastal Garden Route to East London. The woman who answered the phone assured Tebogo that their buffet was still on.

We marched out the same way we came in, without a word or a whinge. Kgaugelo and Maseapo remained seated for a while longer, craving a bit of drama, but eventually gave up when there was no reaction. When they too finally got up to leave, the skinny lady came to them and asked, with a satisfied smirk on her face, "Is there something wrong?" They just looked at her and marched out silently. As they left, an elderly grey-haired man stood up from one of the tables near the entrance and opened the door for them.

"What if the situation is worse at the hotel?" said my friend Mpho, who had come all the way from Limpopo Province for my graduation, as we climbed back into the Kombi.

"We'll have to cross that river with or without a bridge," said my mother.

Despite the restaurant incident, the mood was jovial in our hired minibus. My son, who was in the front passenger seat, kept extending his arm behind him, the way taxi drivers do when they're demanding their fare.

"*A e tle ka disiti*. Bring the money seat by seat with the change sorted," said my son, imitating the harsh tone of most South African township taxi drivers. The others laughed.

"Hey! *Wena*, taxi driver, slow down, man. Our children are still young. We don't want to die in an accident," Mpho imitated a disgruntled taxi passenger.

"Hey mama! If you want to be in control, go buy yourself a car. This taxi is mine. I will drive it the way I want," Tebogo said.

Everyone said something that reminded us of how it was to travel in a township taxi. We did not feel the twenty-kay stretch to the hotel at all. Everyone was laughing all the way. I chuckled until my stomach hurt.

The topic then went back to what happened at Link-up restaurant.

"I knew something wasn't right when I saw the name of the restaurant. Link-up is a chemist, not a restaurant. It's not a good name for a place where people eat. Probably their food wouldn't have been nice. This whole thing must be God's way of saving our taste buds from a disgusting experience," said my mother. Everyone laughed.

"*Mma*, the chemist is Link, not Link-up," said my son.

"You denied me and Maseapo the opportunity to show you our ability to make white people vanish. If we'd stayed a little bit longer, you would have seen us in action," said Kgaugelo.

"*Yaa!* They need to vanish back to Europe or, better, into the sea," said my mother.

"No, *Mma*! Not all of them are bad," said my son. "I have many friends at school who are white and good. When you talk like that, you are now behaving like the Link-up woman."

"Don't remind me of that racist. *Mxe*! That thin, cocky psychopath! She belongs in the ocean with sharks."

After this outburst, all kinds of racist anecdotes came out. My friend Mpho told us about an incident in a Johannesburg restaurant. A white waiter wrote "darkies" on an order slip instead of the table number. This was the only table occupied by blacks in the restaurant. The waiter then accidentally gave the customers the order slip instead of their bill. When they saw this, all hell broke loose, and the customers proceeded to sue the restaurant for discrimination.

I'd also experienced my share of racism. Earlier that same week, a white cashier at a bookstore stopped processing my payment for the books I'd purchased and went to help two white ladies who had just come in. I shouted after her, demanding that she return to finish my transaction. I think I saw a trace of remorse in her eyes after that, but I might have been imagining it. I decided not to mention my incident as now everyone was competing to tell their own stories.

"Let me tell you what happened to me earlier this week at the Game store parking lot in Polokwane," said my mother.

My mother was about to park her car when an Opel Astra simultaneously moved into the space next to hers.

The Astra parked very close to the left border of the parking space, leaving little room for my mother. When she opened her door, it lightly clipped the Astra. She then pulled it back and negotiated her "big mamma" body out of the car. The man who was driving the Astra did not make any effort to reverse and park appropriately. But my mother was in too good a mood to make an issue of it.

The lady in the passenger seat was a slender, elderly white woman. She was able to slide her small figure out effortlessly. Her door did not touch my mother's Mercedes. My mother examined the area where her door had brushed against the Astra, to make sure there was no dent or a mark.

She then felt the need to be kind, and apologized. "I am sorry to have touched your car," my mother said politely.

"Yes, you should be sorry. People like you don't belong in a car. You should be jumping up and down in trees," said the white woman crossing the street with the old man. They disappeared into Game.

My mother told us that she was so shocked by the rude response that at first, she was unable to act. She said it felt as if there were gears grinding in her head and a piece of rotten pork blocking her throat, preventing her from saying anything. When she'd gathered her wits, she decided to go into Game to hunt for the couple so that she could give them a proper response.

"I was not the one in the wrong! They parked too close to me, and I apologized for touching their car, and yet she tells me that I don't belong in a car. She must be mad!"

These were my mother's thoughts as she rushed through the aisles, tracking the elderly couple as if they were criminals. The more she thought about the woman's words, the angrier she became. She finally bumped into them at the turn-off to the fifth aisle. The man was pushing a trolley with two huge bags of dog food. She told us that she could feel the blood flowing through her fists and legs. She was ready to have a boxing match if need be. We all chuckled.

She said she felt her strong rural upbringing emerging and overshadowing her suburban sophistication, the same rage that had propelled her in her youth to fight with boys when they herded cattle and goats in Motupa village. All of a sudden she forgot her position in church as the leading prayer woman and tugged the old lady's grey jersey from the back.

"Hey you! Can you repeat what you said outside, slowly?" my mother said. The woman gave her a look and pulled herself from my mother's grip.

She and her husband rushed rapidly towards the door where the security guards were standing.

My mother followed them, screaming. As she shouted, her voice grew more forceful with every word, her forefinger stabbing the air.

"What do you mean, I don't belong in a car? I want you to know that I do belong in a car, a better car than yours. And the only thing you will ever see jumping in trees are your grandchildren, not me. Why don't you go back to Europe where you come from and leave us in peace?"

By then, everyone in the shop had turned to see what was going on. Some youngsters walked behind my mother, cheering. "Give it to them, Mama! They are disrespectful, these people."

I could imagine how intimidating my mother's powerful, loud voice must have been, because she told us that the couple left their trolley at the entrance without paying. They never reported her to either the manager or the security guards.

"I taught them a good lesson. I know they will never tell a black person to go jump in trees ever again," said my mother proudly.

I wondered if that was true. It's possible that she had planted more hatred in their minds. We listened quietly as she narrated this story. She was so worked up—it was as if she were still at the scene. Raw anger shone from her big round eyes. My son kept on reminding her that not all white people were like that.

"*Mma*, I have many good white friends at school. Don't be fooled to think that all white people hate black people," he said.

My mother's story disturbed me. It was sixteen years after democracy, and yet South Africans were still resentful, tense and bitter towards each other. They were still at each other's necks. When would it ever end? Would there ever be true reconciliation? Maybe with the younger generations, things would be different. I could see it in my son's eyes, that he really believed in what he told his grandmother. But as for the rest of us, we were all closet pessimists. We laughed, but no one commented on the story.

At Fish River Sun, the manageress was also white. She gave us a table and allocated us a waitress straightaway, even though the meal was a buffet. Ten minutes later she said, "You guys look like you're celebrating. What's the occasion?"

"She graduated today." Tebogo pointed at me.

"Oh, no wonder you're dressed so smart," she said, looking at me.

She called one of the waitresses and whispered something into her ear. Two minutes later, we were given two bottles of champagne, on the house. We stayed in the restaurant, chatting, laughing and drinking until all the other customers had left. When the manageress approached our table again to check on us, we panicked. We were embarrassed, thinking that we had overstayed our welcome.

"You're welcome to sit here as long as you want. We're about to close the kitchen, though, so if you need anything you must order now," she said.

When the bar closed, she went out of her way to organize us drinks for the rest of the night. They were brought to us in big silver buckets of ice.

"I must say," announced Tebogo, "that the Link-up experience should not be classified as a race issue. Here we are, twenty kilometers away and treated very differently by a white person. This should tell us something. Maybe it's about being backward. You know, behind the times. *Yaa!* Living in the past. Like a rural person from Limpopo would behave on their first week in Jozi. Give it time," said Tebogo, "things will get better, people will change."

Despite these words, and even in our drunkenness, we could not curb our cynicism. No one spoke: our eyes said it all.

♥

Love Interrupted

Life was different in Modjadji village. In Nobody village, where I came from, the role of a wife and *makoti*, a daughter-in-law, was basically traditional. In this village, being a makoti was as good as being a domestic worker. There was even a song that they sang when they welcomed you as *makoti*: "*mmatswale tlogela dipitsa, mong wa tsona o fihlile*"—mother-in-law, stop doing household chores, the person responsible for them has arrived.

As *makoti*, I was instructed by my mother-in-law to address everyone in the family and all relatives in the plural. The same way Julius Caesar addressed himself as we, us, our and so on. If someone asked me where my mother-in-law was, I had to say, "They went to the shop."

The same went for everyone related to my husband, Leshata, including children. When I shared this with a colleague at work, she said, "My dear, it is not only the family and relatives but also their dogs, cats, goats, and cows."

Nobody really cared about the fact that I was pregnant. I had to do the cleaning, cooking, and washing for all of them. It was back-breaking work. I was willing to go with the flow and be a good *makoti*. Well, *khethile! Khethile!* If you have made a choice, you have to stick to it. If this was the price I had to pay for being with the husband I loved so much, so be it. I was fortunate to have a husband. Most women were struggling to find a man to marry them. Their children were being raised fatherless. *I should be counting my blessings*, I thought.

Little did I know that addressing my mother-in-law in the plural and doing household chores were to be the least of my troubles. I was always tired from having to go to work and then come back home to chores. My swollen feet and stomach cramps did not help.

It is often said that most women marry men that resemble their fathers in character and physical attributes. The only thing my dad and husband had in common was their height. My father was a dignified, humble gentleman. He was the kind of man who always made sure that his family had everything they needed.

"I don't want my children to suffer the way I did," he would say with a somber face. I never heard him raise his voice at my mom, or saw him lay a hand on her. If they ever fought, it must have been behind the closed door of their bedroom.

When I met my husband, I expected him to be of my father's caliber. I was doing my final year at the University of Limpopo, and Leshata was working as a teacher. We met in a queue at Standard Bank, and he charmed the wits out of me. Three months later, I was pregnant. Although I had misgivings about the unplanned pregnancy, he was happy about it. When I told him the news, he wasted no time in making the necessary arrangements. It all started with a letter from his family to mine, informing us of the *lobola* delegation that would be visiting us on the second Saturday of October. Normally it would have been enough just to inform them that I was pregnant and to pay what was called a damage fee. But he insisted on paying both the fee and the *lobola*.

My parents were a bit skeptical about the whole thing. My father reminded me that marriage was a big step and urged me to wait and get to know Leshata better.

"It all happened too quickly. It's just too soon. You have only known him for three months, my girl," said my father.

"It won't help her to wait, the calabash is broken already. She must hurry up and marry, otherwise she will be a *lefetwa*. Who is going to marry her with another man's child? She will grow within the marriage. We will support her," said my mother.

By the end of the year, Leshata had already organized me a teaching post at the primary school in his home village. It was a feeder school for the secondary school where he taught.

I went straight from university to *bogadi*, my mother-in-law's home. We shared a four-roomed house with Leshata's mother, who had never married, and his three younger brothers. His four older sisters were all married and living with their husbands. It was a very uncomfortable situation, as we had only two bedrooms, one for his mother and the other for us, the newlyweds. Leshata's brothers slept in the kitchen on foam mattresses. One of the boys was still at school while the other two stayed at home.

I convinced my husband to build us our own house. With the twins coming, we needed more space. Leshata bought the idea and told me that building a house in the village was not as complicated as it was in urban areas. There was enough space in his mother's yard. He told me that we wouldn't even need an architectural plan. He used a stick to draw lines on the ground and showed the builder how big the rooms should be. The only important thing was that it should be a structure that looked exactly like his principal Moloto's house.

In the ninth month of my pregnancy, I requested that my husband take me to my parents' home, as it was becoming more and more difficult for me to cope with the household chores. I had already started my maternity leave.

"My dear, when you come back with the twins, the house will be finished," said Leshata.

"I will be happy," I said. He had already supervised the laying of the foundation and we had bought all the materials necessary.

It was tradition that when you had your first born, you went to stay with your parents so that your mother could help you with the baby. My mother-in-law agreed.

"Yes, it's Anna's mother who must teach her how to handle her first baby. She can go, it's tradition," she said, planting deposits of snuff into her nostrils, with her head bent backwards. I sat opposite her on a rickety old chair in front of the kitchen table. I stared at her as she wiped the black fluid running from her nose with a grey handkerchief. She spoke as if without her permission I could never go.

Already my mother-in-law and I had had several embarrassing episodes. On Saturdays Leshata would stop me from waking up early, saying I needed some rest. We would lie in bed until nine or even ten in the morning. I would hear my mother-in-law waking up the boys in the kitchen at seven, shouting so that I would know she was addressing me.

"Wake up, wake up, what type of people sleep until this time? You enjoy the sunrays caressing your buttocks, heh? This is not a hotel ... even at a hotel people are up, going for breakfast." Thereafter I would smell cooked porridge, *moroho* being cooked. Then there would be a knock on our bedroom door.

"Leshata! I have something for you, my son," she said.

My husband would jump up, put on his gown, and open the door. "What is wrong mother? We are still resting!"

"*Nxa*! I thought you might be hungry, my son. I brought you some porridge and *moroho*. Here! Take! That school that she is putting you through does not have a break. Take, my son. I don't want you to die of hunger."

My husband came back in with a calabash filled with porridge, dished up in neat, artistic layers, and a yellow enamel plate almost overflowing with *moroho*.

"Leshata, did you hear that? Your mom is insulting me," I said, tears running down my swollen cheeks. I looked at myself in the mirror of the dressing table. I could hardly recognize my ballooned face. The pregnancy had transformed me. My light complexion was gone. I was charcoal dark and my neck and breasts were scaly. I had to sleep with my upper body raised by continental pillows. I knew that the weight I was carrying was abnormal.

"Don't worry about my mom. She is like that. I think it's old age. Let's eat. Mhhh! This looks delicious. You will get used to her. After all, I married you, not her. You don't need to feel guilty. It's me who said you should rest. Don't worry, my dear, just relax," he said.

At home, my mother's tears could have filled a plastic bag when I told her about the situation at my mother-in-law's. "My girl, with the twins, that system of making you their domestic worker just won't work. It's just not on. They think you are a slave. I will find you a domestic worker."

That was to be the cause of my first real fight with my husband. He said he did not believe in domestic workers. When I hired someone, he commanded me to dismiss her immediately.

"My mother is good with children. You won't have a problem with the twins."

My mother-in-law loved children. She was good with them. But still I needed help. The domestic worker issue came between us, and for weeks my husband hardly spoke to me, responding only with "yes" or "no" when I tried to engage him. Interestingly, whenever I seemed at odds with Leshata, my mother-in-law was friendlier to me.

I hired another domestic worker, and this one stayed. After a while he accepted her presence, and things went back to normal. I could see my mother-in-law was not pleased. If she found us laughing together, she would give us an irritated look.

She had now moved permanently with us into our new house. It was a beautiful house, with modern finishings. We had erected a borehole and attached pipes that led into the house, making ours one of the few houses in Modjadji village that had a functional bathroom and a sink in the kitchen. But we still used the outside toilet, as the one inside was not yet properly connected. We had three bedrooms, a study, and a living room, a kitchen with a big pantry, a dining room, and two garages with green doors that matched the green roof tiles.

My mother-in-law helped with the babies. She changed nappies and even washed them (disposable nappies were not popular then). Her helping us meant being with her 24 hours a day. She insisted on sleeping with me to help with the babies at night.

She was the kind of person who bathed properly only once a week. The rest of the time she used about two liters of water in a small bowl to rinse her face daily. Whenever she entered a room, her perfume arrived first. It was a mixture of rotten fish, snuff, and other smells I could not define. I was happy when she got herself a foam mattress. At least I no longer had to share the bed with her. Leshata had to sleep in the other bedroom. That too, I was told, was tradition.

We were always so busy that I hardly had time for my husband. That is when the coming home late started. On some occasions, I did not even hear him return. Most of the time, he came home drunk. Every time my husband came into our bedroom to see the babies, my mother-in-law would rush back in, if she was not already in the room. I did not understand this. She would sit there until he left.

When the girls were three months old, I asked her to go back to her bedroom in the old four-roomed house, declaring that I was now strong enough to cope with the twins.

"Mama, it is now better because they sleep through the night, only waking up for milk," I said to her in a respectful tone.

"No, my girl. For as long as you are breastfeeding, I sleep in here," she said adamantly.

"Why?" I asked.

"It's our tradition. You can't sleep with your husband until you stop breastfeeding. Otherwise you will kill the babies," she said.

"What!" I knew they were expecting me to breastfeed until the twins were at least two. I didn't mind this, as I knew the breastmilk was good for them. Most women in the village breastfed until their children were four or five years old. The child would go and play, then come back and call out loudly, "Mama! Where are you? Come, I want the breasts." Still, I was taken aback about not being able to sleep with my husband for so long.

That evening, I waited for Leshata. He stumbled in at three in the morning. It was pointless talking to him when he was so drunk. The next day, I told him to inform his mother that I no longer needed her services. She could go back to her own room.

After a long struggle, my mother-in-law eventually left. She decided to permanently withdraw all the services she had rendered.

From that day on, my mother-in-law and I became the mouse and the cat. When the twins turned one, I fell pregnant again. I gave birth to a son and my husband named him Moraba. Even then my mother-in-law refused to be involved. When I returned from hospital, Leshata was thrilled that it was a boy. Excited, he called his mother to come and welcome the new member of the family.

"This one, Mma, is going to keep our surname alive," he said, handing the baby to her.

She looked at the boy quietly for a few seconds, with her forehead wrinkled and her torso pulling away from him. "Mh! He does not look like you. Mh! This one is ugly—like a *lekwerekwere* with a big nose," she said, laughing diabolically.

The child began to cry. I grabbed him from her arms, registering my disapproval of her comment.

"What did I do now? I pity you, my son, you have married a mad woman. I hope this madness does not pass on to the children. She can go to hell! I have a right to make whatever comments I like. This child is my grandson, isn't he? She must tell me if it is not yours. I told you I don't like coming into your house. She chased me out when the twins were young."

Leshata did not respond. He picked up the *Sowetan* from the coffee table and sat down to read it as if nothing was going on.

"I see the madness has passed on to you too," she said. "I am talking to you and you just read that useless paper. Let me go to my house. I don't even understand why I was called here. I have more important things to do in my house. Who knows? If I stay longer, this madness might catch me too. *Mxe!*"

My mother-in-law's histrionics no longer touched me. I was used to her now.

After my son turned two, I gave birth to another daughter. My mother-in-law often gossiped with the woman next door, saying, "What can you tell her? My *makoti*, haa! Haa! She knows everything. She is educated. She went to university, *ketsebinki*. She knows it all, yet she makes babies like someone who has never been in a classroom. Ha! Ha! Ha! Like a rat."

In four years, I had given birth to four children. It was hectic raising three toddlers and a newborn. Even with the domestic worker, there was still chaos. When my mother heard that my mother-in-law was not supporting me with the babies, she sent over her sister. My aunt arrived soon after my son's birth to assist me. She was a cripple, her left leg shorter than the right one. When she walked, it looked like she was always about to fall. She was remarkable with all the children.

Aunt Maria had never married and did not have children of her own. She was a humble person, respectful and cheerful. She tried very hard to get along with my mother-in-law, but her efforts were in vain. My mother-in-law remained cold to her. But it was difficult for her to ignore my aunt, because everyone loved her. So infectious was her happiness that people responded with spontaneous smiles when she greeted them. Even the lady next door, who was my mother-in-law's gossiping comrade and drinking mate, adored her.

The tension between me and my mother-in-law intensified. Every time I walked out through the kitchen door, I would find her seated under the marula tree weaving her mats. When she heard my footsteps approaching, she would pause and gather as much saliva as possible in her mouth, then when I came into sight she would spit. The spit would land at my feet and was followed by a sucking sound from her mouth. In African culture, people spit if they see something filthy or smell something unpleasant. That morning I crept towards the kitchen door so that she would not immediately hear my footsteps. I gathered as much spit as I could while still inside the house, and this time I spat first, as she was still marshaling her own saliva. It was a long time before she spat at me like that again.

After the birth of my children, I gained weight, especially around my stomach. I was careful not to wear clothes that were too tight because they revealed my pot belly and love handles. One Saturday, we were going to attend a wedding at Ga-kgapane township, next to the town of Duiwelskloof. I was all dressed up, and even Leshata, who normally didn't compliment me, observed that I looked my best.

When we walked out of the house, our neighbor was hanging her laundry on the washing line, which was close to our yard. My mother-in-law sat under the avocado tree, where Leshata's car was parked. She was eating avocadoes, sprinkling them with salt from a steel side-plate, when she saw us coming. She then called out to her friend, as if she had not seen her for months, "Hey MmaTlou, how are you?" My stomach cramped. I knew her well enough to know a scene was coming.

"I am OK," said the neighbor, her hands moving up and down the line. "Just busy! Lots of washing. These children, they act like they have a servant who will wash their clothes every day. You know we used to wear a dress for a week or two before—"

"You know what, MmaTlou?" my mother-in-law interrupted. "Me? When I was a young woman and I dressed up to go some-where, you could never tell that I had given birth to eight chil-dren. My waist and curves remained where God intended them to be. My tummy was as flat as a fresh virgin's. You would not struggle to tell the difference between my back and my front," she said, raising her voice with every sentence, laughing like someone who had lost her mind. The next-door woman did not laugh or respond.

"Your mom is provoking me. Did you hear that? She is referring to my *mokhaba*. One day I will forget who she is," I said to my husband as we drove away.

"Don't worry about my mother. It's old age. You know how she is," said Leshata. If I were given a rand for every time Leshata gave this excuse, I would have been rich.

♥

Raising my four children became my second job. If I was not at the school, I was breastfeeding or washing nappies or making bottles. I had little time for myself, let alone for my husband. He was also not very good with children. He could not stand the crying and would shout at them to keep quiet, as if he could reason with them like adults. He spent most of his free time away from home, only to return drunk, late at night, when we were all asleep. He would take his dinner plate out of the microwave, eat, and doze off on the couch.

The following morning, he would scream at the twins as they chased each other around the couch: "Hey! Shut up, man! Can't you see I am sleeping?" The twins would be quiet for a while before resuming their play.

One sunny Sunday morning, while I was readying the baby and my son for church, I heard one of the twins screaming. The domestic worker had finished dressing them and was making breakfast for all of us. I jumped up and ran into the living room, with only my petticoat on, to find my husband towing the twins with his right hand. He had unfastened his belt with his left hand and was dragging them into the guest bedroom.

"Hey *wena*! Are you mad? These are children for God's sake!" I screamed at him, trying to pull him away from the children. But his grip was too strong.

"Get out! I am disciplining these rats of yours. I want to teach them how to be respectful. Get out of my way or else I will teach you too," he said. There was such fury and hatred in his eyes, I felt like I was looking at the devil himself. He pushed me with his left hand and laid my babies on the bed as if they were carcasses in a butchery waiting to be sliced. He began to lash them with his belt.

"When I tell you to be quiet, you must keep quiet!" he shouted. Their pink church dresses were flung up, half covering their small faces. The matching panties with frills made their little stick legs appear even thinner.

"Please! Papa! Stop! I will never talk again. I will never in my life talk, Papa. I won't do it again!"

♥

I tried to pull him off. He turned and hit me in the face with the buckled side of his belt and pushed me outside.

I went back into the lounge and Moraba, my two-year-old son, rushed to my side, clinging to my dress. Leshata was now holding the belt in such a way that the buckle was hitting my twins. Their screams killed something in me.

"Mma, stop him! Please stop him!"

"Are you mad? Do you want to kill them?" I screamed.

"*Yaa!* You are the one who spoilt them. I want to teach them good manners while they are still little. I thought I told you to get out," he said, turning the belt on me again.

It felt like I was in a bad movie, or a nightmare, and this wasn't really happening. We all cried: my son, the domestic worker—who was visibly shocked, standing by the door holding the baby—and I. Moraba loosened his grip on my dress. He started hitting his father's legs with his small fists and biting him with his milk teeth. It was only then that Leshata stopped and shouted.

"Take this thing of yours away before I donner it too," he said.

Moraba continued attacking him. The twins escaped from the bed and ran out to their grandmother's house. It was to be the first such episode of violence in our home. I felt like I was a swimmer in a turbulent sea.

I cried the whole day. We did not attend church. My twins remained in their room all day, traumatized. The older one could not walk properly because of the bruises. I could not believe that any sane human being would do such a thing to a child. *Eish! I married a madman*, I thought.

When I called his mother to come and see what her son has done to my children, she said, "Yes, he has to teach them manners while they are still young."

Something in me changed that day. I shut off from Leshata completely. I did not know what else to do. For me a divorce or a separation was not an option, though it was clear that I was married to a borderline case.

That morning after beating the twins, Leshata drove off and was swallowed up by the village, not bothering to return that night. When I went to work the next day, he had still not returned.

The little connection there had been between us was lost. We rarely fought openly or talked to each other. He came and went as he pleased. At times he would stay away for a whole week. The children were happier when he was gone. I felt at peace.

For years, we fought only silent wars, until one night when he had forgotten to take his set of the house keys. I realized this when at two in the morning he hooted from the gate. I had told myself that I was not going to open it for him when I heard a clicking sound. I peeped through the bathroom window and saw his mother with a blanket wrapped around her waist, unlocking the gate. A few minutes later, there was a knock on the front door, and then on the kitchen door, followed by the bedroom window.

"Anna! Anna! Open the door. Where do you think I am going to sleep? Open up! This is my house, you have no right to lock me outside," he said.

I sat on the bed, not responding. If he thought I was going to feed his late-night habits .... I knew that if I opened the door, I would be setting a precedent. One of the twins had woken up and come into my room.

"Mama, someone is knocking," she said.

"Shhh, go and sleep," I said. I walked her back to her bedroom.

Leshata must have knocked for over an hour. His mother also joined him, and they cursed me together. She called me all kinds of things—a mad person, daughter of a wicked witch, a bitch—but I remained silent and kept the lights off. I discovered the following day that he had slept in his car. In the morning, the twins, who were now nine years old, unlocked the front door. To my amazement he did not say anything or shout as usual. He came inside and prepared himself for work as if nothing had happened.

My mother-in-law had more to say: "Who do you think you are? You lock my son outside of his own yard and house. You should be ashamed of yourself. Sis! I am sure this behavior comes from your bewitching mother. I am sure she also locked your father outside. This is my own child that I carried for nine months. If he ever has to sleep outside again, you will know me. I don't think you do." She paused only to spit. I did not respond. She called me every despicable thing she could think of. I waited for her to finish, and when she didn't, I interrupted her, telling her I was late for work. She spat again. That morning her spit could have filled a beer glass.

From then on, my husband spent hardly any time at home. The few times the children encountered him in the mornings, they would tiptoe through the house, careful not to make a sound. Even our dogs were afraid of him. They too were happier when he was not there. When Leshata left through the front door, the dogs would cower in the back yard, and when he came in through the back door, they would hide at the neighbors'. When he was out they would play with my son in the living room or hang around in the kitchen. We always knew when his car was arriving because the dogs would rush outside, as if something were chasing them. My son would pick up his toys and go to his room. Leshata once found the dogs in the living area and kicked them so hard, I swear I heard bones cracking. Even his brothers refrained from playing music at full blast when he was at home.

Everyone was wary of him, except his mother. When she was drunk, she liked to remind people that her son was highly educated. "A teacher, yes, a teacher, came out of me. If there had been school in my time, I would have been a teacher too. This boy has my brains," she would say with pride.

Most Sunday afternoons he brought her a crate of Black Label *magolistos* and drank with her and the woman from next door. You would hear them laughing and talking at the same time.

That Easter Sunday he stayed with them for only an hour before leaving in his car. I greeted my mother-in-law and her friend on my way to hanging the kitchen cloth on the washing line. I was surprised when she returned my greeting without saying anything offensive. *It must be the alcohol,* I thought. I was still smiling when I passed the women on my way back into the house.

"MmaMoraba, there is something I have been meaning to ask you for a long time," she said drunkenly.

I knew there and then that a bomb was coming. I was not in the mood, I was exhausted. I wanted to run into the kitchen, but I could not.

"Tell me," she said enthusiastically, "what happened to that crippled relative of yours. I miss seeing her limping around with the children on her back. Anyway, I am glad she went away because I was afraid for my grandchildren. I had to watch her all the time to make sure she did not fall with them on her back. Ha! Ha! Ha!"

The neighbor didn't laugh. She just gulped her beer from the mayonnaise bottle she was using as a glass.

My mother in-law knew very well that my crippled aunt had died of an asthma attack a year before. She hadn't even attended the funeral. I couldn't understand how she found this a subject for amusement, even in her drunken state. I felt an unusual sensation around my neck, in my chest, then in my eyes, which were now watering. When the feeling got to my hands, I reached for the mop which was hanging on the wall next to the kitchen door. When the mop landed on her head, the first thing to reach the floor was the beer bottle, then her. The crate she was seated on followed. I held the mop in both hands and hit her with all my strength, over and over. Her dress now covered her face, exposing her underwear: a pair of graying cycling shorts. She was as helpless as my twins on the day that Leshata had lashed them. My head was spinning, and I felt my anger rising. I knew then what temporary insanity meant.

"Yoo! Yoo! Someone help. This daughter of a wicked witch is killing me. Yoo! Yoo!" she screamed. I did not let up until her youngest son came out and pulled me away. The woman from next door did not attempt to stop me.

"If you joke about my late aunt again, I will kill you, and I am not joking," I said, walking into the kitchen.

"Aunty leave her. She is drunk," said my brother-in-law.

In the house, I felt my heart in my mouth. I could hardly breathe or talk, but couldn't stop crying—not because she had offended me, but because I could not recognize myself. I had just behaved like my husband.

Leshata came home earlier that day. When his mother heard his car, she ran to meet him at the gate. He parked the car next to the gate and followed her into her house. I knew that I was the subject of their discussion. He only came into our house at about ten that evening. He was surprised to find me drinking tea in the kitchen. Normally by this time, I would be asleep. He took out his dinner from the microwave and sat down opposite me at the kitchen table. I tried to read his face for signs of anger, but there was nothing. He appeared emotionless, although I thought I could sense a gentle sorrow in the lines across his forehead.

The toilet in our house was still not connected, and we all used the pit latrine outside. At night we kept buckets in our bedrooms, which were emptied in the mornings, washed, and then left in the sun until evening. The only time that anyone used the pit latrine at night was for doing a number two. Then you would take the torch we kept in the kitchen and walk outside to where the toilet was situated, about thirty meters from the house.

Following the violent scene with Leshata's mother, I experienced stomach cramps which later complicated into painful diarrhea. I felt I was being punished for hitting the old lady with a mop. I woke up several times from about eleven o'clock, running outside with a toilet roll in one hand and a torch in the other. My long blue night gown swept the leaves and dry grass along the thin path to the toilet. Snakes were not strangers to this path, so I kept my torch close to the ground, to make sure

I didn't step on one. In the toilet, I checked every corner, even underneath the seat.

At about one in the morning, I awoke once more. It seemed the hide-and-seek game with the snakes was going to go on all night. My stomach felt like lightning was striking it from the inside.

I was worried about the interrupted sleep because the next day was a working day. After the last painful visit to the pit latrine, I walked back to the kitchen door. It was locked.

I sat on the front door step for about fifteen minutes, not bothering to knock. It was obvious what was going on. After another fifteen minutes, I went to the twins' bedroom window. I knew they didn't wake easily. I knocked softly. Luckily the older one's bed was next to the window. She opened the curtain.

"It's Mma, don't be afraid," I said softly. She opened the window and I told her to walk quietly to the living room and to open the front door. I then hurried back to the front of the house. My daughter had managed to open the main door but was battling to unlock the security gate. I heard Leshata's voice.

"What are you doing? If you open that door, I will kill you. I want her to know how it feels to sleep outside." He took the keys from my daughter. He looked at me through the bars of the security gate for a few seconds, then laughed, closed the door in my face and locked it.

I sat on the rusting iron-mesh chair on the veranda. It was cold. Small drops of rain began to wet the dry soil. Could this rain not have waited until tomorrow or any other day! *I am definitely being punished*, I thought.

After a while I found myself worrying about the fact that I had run out of toilet paper. And where was I going to sleep? Option A was to wake up my mother-in-law. Given yesterday's drama, that was out of the question. Option B was to go and sleep at a neighbor's house. But I knew they wouldn't open even if I brought Mandela to plead with them—they were all too weary of my mother-in-law. I was thinking about this from the seat of the pit latrine. I must have sat there for over an hour, despite the stench—it was warmer there than on the veranda. But I finally grew tired of the smell and emerged to see lightning cut fiery lines through the sky, which fumed with rain. I got wet just running from the toilet to the kitchen door, almost slipping into the pool of muddy water next to it.

The yard felt unfamiliar that night. The trees that cast shadows during the day now appeared to be closing in on me. The smell of mangoes was everywhere.

"This damn rain," I cursed.

There were still about five hours till daylight. I definitely couldn't survive until morning in these wet clothes. I cursed the rain again, almost as angry with it as I was with Leshata and his mother. Sitting there in my wet gown, shivering, I thought about married life. Why did I get married? I recalled my mother's words: "My girl! You must know that to sustain marriage as a woman, you need a certain level of stupidity." Then I thought about my children and my heart warmed. I knew that my daughter was not going to be able to sleep, knowing I was outside. I went back to her window and tapped softly. This time I had brought my mother-in-law's bench. I climbed onto it and squeezed myself through the open window into my house, like a thief, in front of my nine-year-old twins. They wanted to talk.

"Shhh!" I said, taking off my gown.

In our bedroom, I found Leshata snoring. I deliberately switched my hairdryer on to wake him up. I exaggerated every sound I made to irritate him. He then stopped snoring but did not open his eyes. I knew he was awake. Ten minutes later, I slept.

After that night, drama became the norm in my house. My children grew up not knowing things could be different. Leshata continued to come and go as he pleased, returning drunk. We were now used to it. He would hoot at the gate. It was no longer about him having lost or forgotten to take his set of keys. He was just too lazy to open the gate. His mom or the younger brother would wake up to open for him.

He always managed to announce his return to our in-quisitive neighbors with his blaring hooter. And yet they never complained about the noise. Maybe their husbands were also coming back late. I wished we were living in the suburbs. There the hooting would not have been accepted. The white people or the black diamonds would never have allowed it.

After unlocking the front door, a difficult mission given his drunkenness, he would come inside singing self-composed songs. The one that irritated me the most was the one he sang in Sepedi, about how everyone loves money.

The twins were now sixteen. Sometimes he would wake one of them up and instruct her to bring him his food.

"What's with the long face? I am the head of this family, whether you like it or not. My food must be warmed up," he said. My daughter would heat his food in the microwave and put it on the living-room table for him before going back to sleep. He would eat maybe a piece of meat and then start ranting.

"You cook rubbish. What is this? I know how to cook. I won't eat this rubbish."

I would listen to his staggered movements in the kitchen. He would drop a packet of frozen meat into a big pot, pour wa-ter into it, and place it on the stove to boil, with the packaging still on. Then he would return to the living room, still singing his songs. On some days he played his Zion Church CDs and sang and danced to them until he fell asleep on the sofa. I would wake up, switch off the stove and lights, and put a blanket over him. This was the story of my marriage. It was the same on most of the weekends when he bothered to come home. We were happier when he slept God only knew where.

The battle between father and son started the day Moraba, then 2-years-old, bit Leshata on his legs when he was hitting the twins. My son would not take his father's treatment ly-ing down. He planned and plotted against Leshata's deeds. He dismantled the CD player to prevent him from playing his music at night.

My husband was a superstitious man who believed in African magic and witchcraft. He also believed in the power of the ancestors. One Saturday, while he was raging about his food, my son sneaked out through the kitchen door with a white sheet in his hand. He wore the sheet over his body and knocked on the living-room window when his father began singing his derogatory songs. Leshata had just bought himself a guitar and he was playing along on it.

"Who is knocking on my window? I will kill them," he said in his drunken voice. He then pulled open the curtain and saw a white figure. He screamed like a mad person.

"A ghost! There is a ghost," he cried.

He ran into our bedroom and tried to wake me up.

"Anna! Wake up! There is a ghost," he said.

"Hey *wena*! Leave me alone. There are no ghosts in this house. Are you crazy?" I said, pulling the covers over my head.

He went back to the living room and my son knocked again. I woke up and looked outside through the bathroom window and saw the white figure. I knew it had to be Moraba. He had told me that he had a plan to stop his father from waking us up. He danced and spread his hands in all directions inside the sheet. The white figure moved like an amoeba. It really looked like a ghost when it assumed the different shapes. I laughed and went back to bed. My husband followed me two minutes later. He smelled like a beer hall, but then I was used to the smell. The ghost had sobered him up. He shook me and when I raised my head he said, "MmaMoraba! I am not lying. There is a ghost outside."

"Really! Where?" I said.

"Everywhere, it is a white ghost and it is everywhere."

"Maybe the ancestors were just visiting," I said.

"Why would they visit?"

"I don't know. Maybe they are not satisfied with something. You should have gone out. Maybe they would have told you what they are not satisfied with."

It was strange: it had been so long since we'd had a conversation. That night when I shifted to change my sleeping position, I found his hand wrapped around my body. I knew then that he was really shaken. The following day at five in the morning, he and his mother drove to Shikundu village near the Punda Maria gate to the Kruger National Park. The village, which was 200 kilometers away from our home, was well known for having powerful *inyangas* who were from Mozambique. They went to consult an *inyanga* about the ghost. I was never told the details or outcome of the consultation, but complaints about my cooking stopped.

And then he left for good, taking his salary with him. I later heard that he was living with a woman who was almost half his age and who had four children (not his). This woman was unemployed. I figured that he felt his financial services, and all his other services, were more needed there.

The twins and Moraba were now in tertiary institutions, and my last born was boarding at a private secondary school. I did all I could to put them through school. It became very difficult when the twins were in their final year and Moraba was in the middle of his second year at Wits University. I realized during the second term that I was not going to be able to pay for all three of my children's education. I decided to negotiate with Moraba to come back home and take a break for six months. He would resume his studies the following year when the twins had completed their engineering degrees

The one positive thing about my husband's moving out was that my relationship with my mother-in-law improved. I was no longer the daughter of a wicked witch. That title was taken by Leshata's new woman. I was told that when my mother-in-law was drunk she went to the woman's house and ranted: "You are an uneducated bitch who has stolen my son from his family. I carried him for nine months alone," she said. "If he dies in that shack you call a home, I will make sure you cook him and eat him because you are eating all his money now."

My mother-in-law offered her meager pension money to help with pocket money for the children. I refused to take it but she always gave them something secretly when they went back to school.

Moraba decided to come home a month before the time he was due to return. He had decided to take things up with his dad, as usual. He investigated and found out where his father was staying and went to confront him. But Leshata was out, and Moraba left a note telling him that he needed to see him urgently.

The following day, while I was having my morning tea before going to work, the kitchen door opened and Leshata blasted in like a storm, primed for a fight. He looked shockingly thin, with unkempt hair. His clothes were faded and he smelled of cigarettes and dissatisfaction. He started screaming without even greeting me.

"Where is he? Who does he think he is? He thinks he is a man now and he can go about this whole village looking for me," said Leshata.

"Are you going mad? What are you talking about, Leshata?"

"Why didn't I think of this? You are the one behind it all. Where is he?" he said, walking down the passage that led to the bedrooms. Moraba had heard the commotion and come out of his room.

"Hey *wena*, who do you think you are? You run around the whole village hunting me like I am a criminal," Leshata said.

"I am your son. I have every right to look for you. I want money for my school fees."

"Why didn't you tell your mother instead of going after me like some animal? I am here to warn you. You must stop this rubbish of hunting me," he said.

"Or what? My mother can't afford to pay for all of us. I am told that I have to stay home for six months in the village doing nothing when you are alive and working," said my son.

"I don't have money. What do you want me to do, kill

myself? I don't have money," said Leshata, raising his voice even louder when he said the word "money."

I was watching them from the kitchen table. The next moment my son had pushed my husband into the wall, pummeling him with hard fists non-stop on his head, face, and torso. It was as if he were a punching bag. The boy was far stronger than his father, and when Leshata attempted to hit back, his fists flailed helplessly. Alcohol had finished him.

Then my husband was on the ground, with blood pouring from his face, and the boy began kicking him. I screamed, begging him to stop. The more I screamed, the harder he kicked. I grabbed Moraba from behind. Leshata was also pleading with him to stop. He promised he would get him the money.

"Anna, stop him, this boy will kill me," Leshata screamed.

"*Ngwanaka*, stop. Please, I beg you," I said.

My son now turned his anger on me. "Don't try to stop me, otherwise I'll beat both of you. You are not the one who has to sit here for six months doing nothing when he is using his money to feed all the whores in this world. That is why he is like this, because you don't do anything. You just leave him."

I screamed, "*Yoo, nna mmawe!*"

That's when he stopped. He was crying too. "I want that money by Monday or else I'll come and fix you again where you are staying." He then went out through the front door.

I helped my husband to stand and advised him to try African Bank. They could give him a loan which would be deposited into his bank account in a day or two.

"How much do you need?" he asked.

"If you can get five thousand rand, that will help."

"OK," he said meekly, his eyes protruding abnormally.

The following day, he brought the money. I was watching TV with my son when he came in. He put the envelope on the table without a word and walked out.

"I am leaving tomorrow," said my son. "I want you to move back home. When I come for winter vacation, I better find you here. If I don't, I will come find you again, and I will hit you and all the people you are living with."

"That's enough. You don't talk to your father like that. I will throw you out of my house," I said, but my husband was already gone. I realized that I had not only married a madman, I had also given birth to one.

A week later, my husband came back home. I was not fully convinced that it was because of my son's threats. I suspected that things were no longer so at his other home.

This time it was just the two of us in our house. With the children at school, I was prepared to work on the marriage. *Marriage! Was it worth all the trouble?* I wondered. I needed to stick to my marriage vows. What else could I do, really? No man would marry me with four children. And single life was not appealing, because people just didn't respect women who were not married.

Leshata and I both carried a lot of pain. I dealt with mine by feigning indifference. That made things worse. He tried to drown his in alcohol, but it seemed the pain had learned how to swim.

Then we found church. I wasn't sure if it was merely a crutch, but things began to change. Leshata stopped drinking and being abusive. And I no longer had to pretend to make my marriage work. But all I had to bank this rebirth of my marriage on was hope and faith.

Lebo's Story 1: A Young Girl's Dream Interrupted

The fact that Lebo was born into a poverty-stricken family did not prevent her from having ambitions. She never met her real father. She was conceived when her mother was 15-years-old and raised by her grandparents while her mother worked as a live-in domestic in the suburbs of Nelspruit.

Lebo had always been a dreamer. She'd always believed that she was not meant for a mediocre kind of life. Her mother, the first born, was conceived when Lebo's grandmother was thirteen. At that time, she was working as a kitchen girl on a farm outside Sabie. Lebo's mother had also never known her real father and was raised by a step-father from Malawi.

Lebo and her mother lived in a three-roomed shack with her two uncles and aunt. Every day after school she went to her teacher's home to help with household chores and the baby. She was only 8-years-old but could handle any task, including cooking. At teacher Mangena's home, she got to enjoy luxuries such as sitting on a real sofa and watching television. She got to eat "Sunday food" every day. It was a surprise to her that people could eat vegetables and meat more than once a week.

For Lebo to enjoy these things, she performed every task to perfection. Teacher Mangena acknowledged that Lebo was better and faster than the domestic worker she was paying. When the baby was with Lebo, teacher Mangena would forget that there was a baby in the house, and was only reminded by the occasional giggle. This ability to soothe the baby earned Lebo the privilege of being allowed to sleep over sometimes.

Lebo's grandmother did not have any problem with this

arrangement. In fact, she went around boasting to everyone. "Lebo is now teacher Mangena's child. She is there all the time. My grandchild is living like a white man there. Did you know they eat meat every day in that house? Maybe they will take her to the big school when she finishes matric."

At teacher Mangena's house, Lebo got her first taste of the high life. She marveled at the toilet and the taps in the bathroom. Using toilet paper instead of newspaper was an unimagined luxury for her. The few times that she went home, the whole family would sit around listening to her.

"The toilet is in the house. You just go, close the door, and do your thing," said Lebo.

"What! In the house! What happens when you do a number two? You are lying ... No! Not in the house ... What about the smell?" asked her uncle, who was two years older than her. They all laughed.

"Even number two, you do it in the house. There is a small well inside. You pull a handle and the water comes down and cleans everything out of the toilet. It is not like the pit toilet where everything stays in there and stinks. They even have a perfume in the bathroom in case there is a small smell."

Most of all Lebo loved sleeping on the soft bed with the smooth shiny sheets and blankets. She could not believe the softness. She was used to sleeping on the ground, on woven mats, with only a thin grey blanket.

When the teacher was not home, Lebo would act as if the house were hers and walked around imitating teacher Mangena's movements and way of speaking, lacing every sentence with an English word.

Most nights Lebo lay awake fantasizing about her future. In her vision, her house would have another one on top—like the one in *The Bold and the Beautiful*—and a swimming pool. She saw herself as a business lady with lots of money, walking around in high heels giving orders. She fell asleep to these fantasies, and at times they crossed over into her dreams. Sometimes she dreamed she was laughing and having lunch with the people she saw on television. Then she would be woken up by a mosquito or her aunt's leg crossing over hers. She'd lie awake, furious to be wrenched away from the world she felt she belonged to.

When she turned twelve, she visited her mother at her workplace in Nelspruit. The first thing that startled her was the dog house that was next to her mother's cottage. *A dog with a house—that is insane*, she thought. The dog's blanket looked exactly like her grey blanket back home, only it was thicker and newer.

After helping her mother to unpack groceries, Lebo picked up the till slip. She added the money spent on Husky, Whiskas, tinned pet food and Bob Martin tablets. These cost more than her family spent on groceries at home. The big black fridge was unbelievable to her. *The first thing I will buy when I get rich is a fridge like this one*, she thought. She wondered why the white people were so thin when there was so much food in the house. She asked her mother about this.

"It's that red wine that they drink with their food. Madam says it eats up all the food and makes them thin," said Lebo's mother. Lebo was not impressed. She hated alcohol. She had never known anyone who drank to be responsible.

The house was the type she owned in her fantasies. It was a double-story with huge windows, but there were no curtains in most of the rooms. They did not have the bridal-dress-like voile that Lebo's teacher had in every room. Instead, they had grass-like panels hanging in the windows. You had to use strings to open them and close them. After a while Lebo learned how to operate them, and whenever she got a chance she would pull on the strings, fascinated by how they opened and closed.

Her mother was shocked by how much Lebo knew about housework and cooking. She could make all sorts of dishes, from lasagna to Greek salad. The white family was impressed and preferred Lebo's cooking to her mother's.

When she was done cleaning, Lebo would run around with a towel and pantyhose, rubbing all the mirrors and shiny surfaces until they gleamed. Her mother made her wear one of her overalls with a matching head scarf. The spinach-colored uniform hung loose on the young girl. She looked like a tent pole in it.

Lebo had her mother's peachy complexion but her hair was not as fluffy. Her beautifully crafted braids escaped in places from the scarf and her big round eyes were accentuated by long eyelashes. Even in the ugly, oversized overall, her beauty could not be concealed.

The madam once told her that she was pretty. "You are like a white person dipped in chocolate," she said.

Every time Lebo heard the madam's car coming, she would run to the garage and sweep the ground. Then she would stand by the car licking her forefinger shyly while she waited for them to get out. With her ready smile, she carried their bags or whatever they had brought with them into the house.

"Oh shame! Maria must stop making you wear that thing," said the madam.

Lebo found it strange that they all called her mother by her first name. In her village it was rare to find adults called by their first names. It was regarded as disrespectful. They would rather call you by your child's name—like MmaLebo or PapaLebo.

Another thing that bothered her was how the two sons, one her age and the other a year older, never talked to her. They treated her as if she were invisible. *One day they will wish they'd been friends with me*, she thought. When she cooked meals for them, she was sometimes tempted to spit on the food to get revenge. Every now and then, they would come to the servants' quarters after hours and shout from outside.

"Maria!"

"Yes, what can I do for you?" her mother said.

"Did you wash my black tackies? I can't find them in my room."

Her mother would then hurry back to the main house to look for them. Lebo was surprised at how dependent the boys were. When her mother came back, she said, "*Mma*, when I am rich, my children won't be like these boys. They don't even know how to wash their own underwear."

"Dream on, my girl. Your children will wash underwear because there will be no one to wash them for them. You will never be rich. If it was that easy, we would all be rich. These people did not become rich by themselves. Their grandparents' grandparents were also rich. And *wena*, who has ever been rich in your family? You are going to follow the same road as me and your grandmother. You can't escape it. The sooner you accept that, the better. I am just happy that you are not lazy: you know the white man's work. Your children won't die of hunger."

"Don't compare me to you! I am not you. I am going to have a business. You will see—I am going to be rich like them."

"Ha!" her mother laughed, shaking her head.

From that day on, Lebo stopped sharing her ambitions with her mother. In the evening when they were in the servants' quarters, she would watch television rather than talk. *My mother will never see things the way I do—that is why she is poor*, Lebo thought.

The cottage her mother lived in was very comfortable— better than their shack. There was a bath with a shower at the top and hot water. There was a two-plate stove with an oven and a grocery cabinet in the corner. This was something that was not in teacher Mangena's house.

In one corner there was a stack of boxes. Lebo's mother collected all kinds of things that the white people threw away— ice cream containers, mayonnaise bottles, almost finished toothpaste, magazines. Lebo felt sorry for her mother. She understood that this was the result of never having had much. It led to an inability to let go of things, even when they were useless.

In one of the boxes, there was a tray where she dried all the leftover bread and rolls. Whenever she went home, she brought boxes full of dried bread cut into the shape of rusks. For a week the family would have a break from eating porridge in the mornings with their tea.

Lebo was at her happiest on the nights when her mother went out. She would leave after watching *Generations*, and return the next morning at five. "I am going to get some fresh air," she would say before leaving.

On the day Lebo arrived, her mother had introduced her to Uncle Peter, who was the gardener next door. She wondered if her mother's disappearance had something to do with him.

Many things fascinated Lebo at her mother's work. In the two weeks she spent there, she learned a lot about the high life. Until then she had daydreamed of owning a business but had had no idea what type. The white family's gardener, Olwethu, told her that the boss was an engineer and owned a construction company. He also owned trucks that transported things to faraway places. Olwethu told her that the boss was making a lot of money. There and then, Lebo decided that this was the company she would have. She wondered why her mother's boss could not build her mom a three-roomed house. It would cost him nothing: he had lots of money. She wondered if the white family knew they stayed in a shack. Her mother had worked for them for eleven years, but they didn't even know where she lived.

One weekend during Lebo's visit, the family went away. She walked around in the main house giving instructions to invisible servants, acting as if she had owned the place and she was the madam. She kissed an imaginary husband.

"Hello darling. *Nxa*! How was your day, my love?" She then turned and took a glass from the shelf and said, "Maria, this glass is not sparkling. Come, go wash it again." She walked as if she were wearing high heels, poking the countertops with her finger. "Hey, you have not dusted. What is this?"

She stood in front of the glass doors on the patio and watched herself in their reflection, talking like the madam. She was fascinated by the madam's behavior. It resembled that of the people she saw on TV. They kissed and said I love you openly.

It surprised Lebo because in her village the only people who kissed in public were the drunk girls at the tavern. And even with them, it was not that common. She more or less lived with teacher Mangena and her husband, but she had never seen the two kissing or heard them saying I love you to each other.

It seemed that Lebo's mother had picked up her madam's ways. "I love you, my girl," she would say after a conversation with Lebo on the phone. For a while it had disturbed her a lot. She thought her mother must be dying or something. It was a relief to finally understand where it came from.

Lebo lived in a world of her own. She lived for tomorrow. Before she went back home, the madam gave her five hundred rand and some clothes that she no longer wore. Lebo was happy. It was the first time that she had earned money and it felt good. But this was just the beginning—she was going to earn a lot more.

Everyone was happy to see her when she returned home.

"Ah Lebo, you are working for *lekgowa* for just two weeks and already you look like them. *Bona*, you are more yellow than when you left," they teased her at home. She could not wait to see teacher Mangena. After telling everyone the Nelspruit stories, she left for the teacher's house.

"Look at you. You have gained weight. As if we don't feed you here. My children missed you a lot," said teacher Mangena.

Lebo laughed and told her everything. "I now know how to make cheese, mushroom, and white sauce. I know how to bake carrot and black forest cake and many types of muffin. Tomorrow I will bake the carrot cake for your children. I bought the ingredients with the money I earned," Lebo said.

"*Eish*, you came at the right time. There are some clothes that need to be washed. Check the basket in the bathroom," she said.

Over the years, Lebo's constant smile and work ethic allowed her to continue to enjoy the comforts of the wealthy people for whom she labored. When she was fifteen, she was invited to live with the teacher's sister, Sindi.

"I like this girl. She is effective and clever. She can help me with the children when I am on call. I can find her a school," said Sindi when she visited teacher Mangena from Johannesburg.

After informing Lebo's grandmother, Sindi took Lebo with her back to her home. Sindi and her husband were both doctors. Although Lebo missed home a lot, at first she was content in Johannesburg. However, things became complicated a year after her arrival.

At sixteen, Lebo was now ripe with hips; a firm, beautiful behind; and neat, well-poised breasts. There was a lovely rhythm in her hips that made her skirt swell out and sway around her as she walked. At home, although a lot of the boys in the village tried their luck with her, she wasn't interested. She did not have the time to spare them, as she was always at the teacher's house. She knew that if she ran after boys, her dream of being rich would evaporate like frost when the sun came out. She would fall pregnant and have to work full-time as a domestic worker. Teacher Mangena told her that there would be plenty of time for boys when she finished school and became a teacher. She told Lebo that she would meet a perfect husband like hers. Lebo never discussed her dream to have her own company with her teacher.

During one of her mother's visits, Lebo's mother's boss asked her what she wanted to do when she finished school. She told him that she wanted to start her own construction business. He laughed. "Honey! Listen to this," he called out to his wife. "Mary wants to go into the construction business."

"She had better work hard. Maybe someday wishes will indeed be horses," said his wife, laughing. They had given her a new name. The madam said the name Lebo confused her and it was difficult to remember. She decided on Mary.

"Mary the businesswoman," said the boss sarcastically, shaking his head.

Lebo was taken aback. She did not understand his mockery, but from that day on, she decided to keep her dreams to herself.

In Johannesburg, she worked hard to please, as usual. By this time, her ready smile was misinterpreted by her new boss, Lucky Mabuza, Sindi's husband. Lebo hero-worshipped both of them. They gave her hope. Looking at them and all that they had, she knew it was possible to be successful.

She looked up to Lucky even more because he too came from a poor family in KwaZulu-Natal. On the nights when Sindi was on call, Lebo would serve Lucky supper. Then she bathed the children and put them to bed.

"Lebo! Lebo!" Lucky called her one night from the living room. It was quiet in the house.

She ran to him.

"*Buti* Lucky," she said with her radiant smile.

"Please make me some tea."

"Rooibos or Five Roses?" Lebo asked.

"No, chamomile. You'll see it. It's a yellow box," said Lucky.

"OK."

Lebo was already in her black satin pajamas and the morning gown that madam had given her. She brought the tea in a white pot with warm milk and white sugar in a bowl. It was all neatly presented on a tray covered with a white cloth. She knelt down and put the tray on the glass coffee table in front of him.

As she knelt in front of him, transferring things from the tray to the table, she noticed him watching her, his gaze falling on the gap between the buttons of her pajama top. She felt her cheeks burning, and quickly pulled the top closed.

"Sit down," he said to her.

She wondered if she had done something wrong. It had never crossed her mind that he could be attracted to her. In her opinion, people like him didn't find poor people like her attractive—not when he had a wife who was a doctor. One day is one day. *When she was rich, she would date men like him,* Lebo thought. Who knew? Maybe even better than him. She looked at Lucky with questioning eyes.

"Did I do something wrong, *buti*?" she asked.

"No, my girl, I just wanted to talk to you," said Lucky. She was glad, because she wanted to ask him about how he'd managed to escape the poverty that he was born into. He asked her what she wanted to do after she completed Grade 12.

She looked into his eyes and saw compassion. *This is someone who will understand my dreams*, she thought. Despite her resolve not to share her ambitions with anyone, she told him everything, and he seemed impressed. For the first time, someone believed she could do it.

"You can be anything you want to be. What you need is education," he said. He told her that she should focus mostly on the commerce stream. Then she asked him how he'd managed to study at university. He told her about the *bursaries* and grants he'd been given. He also said that the government had provided grants to help young people start their own businesses. He opened up his laptop and showed her the Umsobomvu Youth Fund and Kula trust websites. It was the first time she had touched a computer. Even though she was not operating it, she read the information and he showed her the buttons for scrolling. She felt important. After a while he asked her if she had a boyfriend or if she had ever had one.

"I think boys will spoil my future. I will have a boyfriend when I'm done with school and have started my own business," she said.

"That is why I am asking you. I wanted to warn you about them. They are dangerous. When you are here, you are safe. But when you are at home, you must look after yourself."

That night, they both did not sleep. Since Lebo had come to Johannesburg, it had been difficult for her to fantasize the way she always had while she was at home. Possibly this was because there was more work in Sindi's house, so she was always tired when she went to bed and fell asleep straight away. Or it could have been the fact that there were no mosquitoes here and the bed was comfortable. But that night she lay awake thinking about all the information *buti* Lucky had given her. And her heart was warmed by the fact that he believed in her dreams.

This was how their friendship started. Lucky no longer scheduled his night shifts to coincide with hers. He would come back home, wait for Lebo to take the children to sleep, and then they would have their chat. They talked for hours over chamomile tea. Some days he would bring a few beers and drink them while she drank the tea.

Lebo's admiration grew with each day they spent talking. She saw him as a redeemer, the most knowledgeable man she had ever met. She thought he was cleverer even than her mother's boss.

Lucky's mother had also been a domestic worker. "My mother worked for white people her whole life but died poor. The family she worked for did not even come to her funeral," he told Lebo.

They shared jokes about the white people their mothers had worked for. He had worked as a gardener for his mother's bosses. Lebo tried to hide the new feeling she felt for *buti* Lucky. She remained respectful to his wife, even though Sindi was cold to her most of the time. She was so different from teacher Mangena. Sindi worked Lebo like a slave. As the children were very young, this meant that Lucky was her only friend in the household. At times they would go for weeks without having their talks. During that time she would go over the last conversation they'd had, eagerly anticipating the next chance they would get to speak. Some mornings he would stand next to her at the kitchen sink, rinsing his favorite coffee mug. When he turned, their sides touched. She felt a thrill which she could not explain.

One night when Sindi was on call, Lucky came home drunk after an evening spent with friends at the Market Theatre. On arriving home, he went straight to Lebo's room. He told her that he was in love with her, that he'd felt this way since the day she'd arrived. He promised her that he would help her achieve her dreams because he loved her. He would redeem her from her poverty. He made her all the promises that every man who wants sex will make.

Drunk as he was, Lucky stated his case in a dignified way. He quoted Shakespeare and poets she had never heard of. That night he slept in Lebo's room. His rounded belly, a sure sign of middle-age indulgence, spread across the single bed.

Lucky did not last a minute before it was all over. He didn't know whether to blame the alcohol or overexcitement. He promised her that it was going to be better the next time. Lebo was not aware that it had not been good. She didn't know how it should have been; it was her first time. In the morning she watched him sleeping with his mouth open, snoring loudly. She woke him up to go to his room as Sindi would be coming home soon and the children might wake up. This was the beginning of their affair, which went on that way for three years.

Most mornings Lucky waited for Sindi to leave and then spent an hour with Lebo before going to work. Lebo was puzzled by his unchanged behavior when Sindi was around. It didn't seem like he was pretending to act natural. He was as if there was really nothing going on. In contrast, Lebo felt an intense sense of guilt and awareness of their betrayal. As much as her affection for Lucky grew, she was always aware that she was taking the caresses and closeness that belonged, by law, to another woman.

Lucky became incredibly possessive, allowing Lebo to go home only when he and Sindi went to visit his in-laws in Hazyview. Even then he would sneak out to check if she was at her grandmother's. He would bring groceries for Lebo's family—a bribe they were happy to accept. He brought more food than they were able to buy in a month. Amongst other things, there would be fresh bread, something they ate no more than ten times in a year. Although Lebo's grandmother received him warmly, she would say, "This man thinks I was born yester-day. I can see what he is up to. You must be careful. If the wife finds out, she will kill you with her bare hands or *muti*."

"What are you talking about, *koko*? That man is my boss," Lebo said.

"I am not an idiot. Anyway, who knows? Maybe he will take you to university when you finish *matric*."

A few months went by, when one September morning Lebo realized that she had not had her period in four months. Worried, she sent a text message to Lucky. He called her immediately.

"Why did you wait for so long to tell me?" he said.

Lebo had not been happy for some time. She was beginning to feel disillusioned by Lucky. He was no longer paying her so much attention. Her fantasies now seemed far-fetched. She was eighteen and she was in love with a man who could never be hers.

"I will arrange for you to get an abortion at Marie Stopes Clinic," he said.

"I will never have an abortion! My mother didn't abort me at fifteen and I won't kill a child," Lebo said.

"That is because when your mother conceived you, abortion was illegal," he said. "You know you can't keep that child. What about your dreams? This child will ruin your future. You will end up a domestic worker like your mother and grandmother."

Lebo was disappointed. She wanted him to be happy and to tell her that he would support her and the child. Now she doubted him. He had used her innocence to get what he wanted. He told her that if his wife ever found out, it would be the end of her!

"You can look forward to a life of washing dishes and cleaning shit inside other people's toilets," he said.

She refused to have the abortion and he didn't touch her again. She told Sindi a boy from home was the father. Lucky tortured her by flaunting his love for his wife. On Saturdays, he would shout for her to bring them coffee and breakfast in bed. She would find them snuggling under the covers. She missed her grandmother's three-roomed shack. When she returned home in December, she found that the new four-roomed house her mother had been building was completed.

She was angry with both Lucky and herself. She felt tempted to spill the beans, but resisted the urge. She feared the pregnancy might be the end of her dream. *No, I won't let it be*, she thought. She buried herself in books, preparing for her matric exams. After the exams, she went home for good. She avoided teacher Mangena because she felt guilty and ashamed.

When she told her grandmother about the pregnancy and Lucky's reaction, the old lady said, "I am happy you did not kill the baby. If he does not want to be involved, leave him. Don't force him. The child will grow. It will not be the first child to be rejected. Look at you: you didn't die from not having a father. And you are now a full-grown woman."

Lebo passed *matric* and gave birth to a baby boy on New Year's Day. She found a job as a receptionist at a lawyers' firm. To her grandmother and her mother, this was the best job. They praised God with so many words, thanking him for elevating their daughter, who had been abandoned by the father of her child.

"God is better than witches," said Lebo's grandmother.

As for Lebo, the job was a bridge to her dream. At the lawyers' practice, when it was not busy, she spent her time daydreaming and researching the construction business.

One day my dream will come true. One day is one day, she thought.

Lebo's Story 2: It's My Turn to Eat

Her whole life, Lebo had felt like she was walking in waist-high sand, as if she were dreaming the right dreams at the wrong time and having a blind date with the future. Now it was the right time. Lebo no longer had to swallow things.

Her grandmother would tell people, "My granddaughter is richer than the white people. When I go with her to do shopping, she pays with a small yellow card and they give her everything we have bought. She told me she is going to buy her mother's boss's house. God is really better than witches. Look, she has built us such a big house with a tile roof. You can't hear the rain from inside the house. Really, it is a miracle."

She went on and on, telling neighbors, teachers, and anyone who would listen. "I'm afraid that people will bewitch her. You know when she buys groceries, she buys in boxes—as if she wants to put the shop out of business. She even stopped her mother from working," Lebo's grandmother said, with signs of distress on her face.

Reactions among the people of Mandelaville varied. The educated, mostly nurses and teachers, wanted to know if Lebo ever finished her tertiary education. Some asked where she was getting the money from, insinuating that it might have been acquired illegally. Others watched out for her car when she came to visit her grandmother and asked her to hire their children or connect them to whatever she was doing.

"The cows must graze heading home. You can't eat out there alone. You must not forget those you grew up with," they would say. Wealth is revered in poor villages. Lebo had gone from being a young woman who used to do her teacher's laundry to get a decent meal to a demigod in the eyes of the villagers. She now had her own construction business and a fleet of cars, graders, tractors, and trucks. Every now and then she brought a grader to re-gravel the road to her grandmother's place. She said the road was not good for her new Volvo. Children and adults gathered around her cars when she came to the village to attend funerals and other important happenings. Some asked her about her company. A young girl or boy would say, "*Aus* Lebo, how is the construction business? Can you give me tips on how I can get into it?"

"If anyone comes to you and says they want to get you into the construction business, you must run. It is not easy. You work like a slave," was Lebo's usual response.

She never missed occasions where she knew her former teachers would be present. She loved the look in their eyes when they saw her. Every time she arrived in a different car. Sometimes she would hire one just to arrive in a car they did not know.

She loved it when one of the male teachers would comment, "That is a big machine for a young girl. It is for old men like me. But you know teaching—the government does not pay much. I will probably buy it with my pension money."

"That is why I never wanted to be a teacher, because I like nice things," said Lebo. Money had done more than make Lebo rich: it had changed her, and not only for the good. Most people in the village gradually distanced themselves from her, sensing her world to be disturbingly far from theirs. She spoke to people as if they had no feelings, revealing their weaknesses in front of everyone. But the villagers let her get away with it because she had money.

Lebo's mother was now married to Uncle Peter, her gardener boyfriend. She had three other children. Lebo bought her a six-roomed house in Shatale township, where she lived with her family. She also bought a van for them. She advised them to sell fruit and vegetables to hawkers in the township. When she came to visit them, they jumped around to make sure they got all the things she liked. These were simple things like fat cakes from the market, chicken feet with sour porridge, and Fanta Orange. Lebo's step-father used to be abusive towards her mother when he was drunk, but after he got the van he never laid hands on her again. Lebo paid a driving school to teach him how to drive, and he was now a successful fruit hawker in the township, his gardening days behind him.

"I am the first in my family to have a car," he boasted.

Lebo liked him because he provided a father figure for her. She felt she was like her friends in Nelspruit now, who always talked about their fathers.

Three years earlier, she had enrolled in the Seda Learnership Programme, a government initiative to empower the previously disadvantaged to own construction companies. They were trained for six months and given small contracts for a year before moving on to do their own thing. From the group of thirty trainees, she was the only one who was doing well. With most of the new business owners, Seda had to intervene to save them from bankruptcy. When they received payments for their first jobs, a lot of them became extravagant. They bought cars and rented houses in town instead of paying bills and saving for the next project. Many of them fell into the habit of eating out and entertaining friends several times a week. They also spent a lot on designer clothing. The next thing they knew, they could not even pay their workers and ended up doing shabby construction work on the project given to them.

Lebo was fortunate because when she started her business, she had been approached by her mother's boss, who proposed they work together. His business was not doing well because construction jobs were now being allocated in accordance with black economic empowerment policies. White males were classified as previously advantaged. Lebo had always known that she would succeed one day, but she'd never imagined being in a position where her mother's boss would be at her mercy. It took her a week to respond to his request. She consulted an *inyanga* and her priest.

They both assured her that it was a good move because the white man was experienced. They warned her not to let him handle all financial issues. She agreed to do business, on the condition that he would sell her his house if they made profit of five million each. The deal was sealed. Lebo brought in one of the lawyers from the firm where she'd worked as a receptionist to draw up a contract.

From then on Lebo was worshipped not only by the people from her home village, but also the family her mother worked for, whose house she used to clean on visits during school holidays. The two brothers who used to treat her as if she were invisible were now able to sit at a dinner table and attempt small talk. She told them they had it easy studying in their mother tongue at Stellenbosch University.

"If I could learn in my mother tongue, I could finish a four-year degree in two," she said. *Now their study fees come from my deals and they are warming up to me*, she thought.

When she went into partnership with their father, he was deep in debt and his business was about to go down. Having Mr. Piet de Kock as a silent partner proved to be a wise business decision. He handled most things—the admin work, marketing, and overseeing the construction work. Lebo handled the recruitment of staff, the finances, and also showed her face when necessary at site inspections and government meetings. Piet was a qualified engineer and knew a lot more about business management. He coached her on the ins and outs of running a successful business and on which tenders were available. She would use her charm or even pay the *tshotsho* to secure them. They were a good team. Money flowed in and, unlike with most inexperienced black contractors, the jobs were well done. The De Kock family now regarded Lebo as one of their own.

"Lebo is my god-sent daughter. We work well together," said Piet when people asked questions about how they came to be so close. He was always animated when he mentioned this, as though he needed to prove his open-mindedness to himself. It was important for his survival not to project himself as the kind of white person that saw black people as idiots. For every deal, they went fifty-fifty. In less than two years, they had both profited more than eight million each. Lebo had earned herself a good reputation and an award from the Department of Transport.

In Nelspruit, which was an hour's drive from her home village, Lebo was not the only rich young person. Her grandmother agreed with her that it was the best place to live, even though their reasons were not the same. Lebo thought it was good for business while her grandmother was happy that people wouldn't bewitch her there because they didn't know about her poor background.

The scars of her difficult childhood remained with Lebo, denying her complete happiness and peace. Her life mostly revolved around proving a point, to both those who had undermined her in the past and those who still attempted to do so.

I have to discipline those people who look down on me by showing them that they are nothing, she often said to herself. The fact that she did not have tertiary education did not make it easy for her. In Nelspruit most people were highly educated and at times in social setups they would have clever conversations about politics and economics. She did not participate for fear of appearing stupid. She just smiled and nodded a lot. She told all her new friends that she was an engineer by profession. At times she believed that some people who were jealous of her initiated these conversations to make her feel excluded. She told Piet about this and asked him how she could overcome this problem, and especially the fact that she still misused tenses when she spoke English. She desperately wanted to fit in. Piet, who also was not a first-language English speaker, understood. He arranged for the woman who used to tutor his boys when they were at secondary school to give her lessons, and advised her to read newspapers and books.

Having purchased Piet's house, she felt the need to flaunt it—to show how far she had come. She hired an interior decorator (a friend of Piet's) who recommended repainting the house in fashionable earth colors. A painter, another of Piet's connections, was contracted to do the job. She spent two hundred thousand rand on new furniture. She transformed the kitchen and changed the cabinets from oak to black with a grey marble finish.

She also bought a black double-door frost-free fridge. The servants' rooms were almost the size of a normal house. Lebo was the kind of person who acknowledged the humanity of those who served her, and her helpers were well provided for.

Once everything was set up, she decided to host a house-warming party. She invited everyone that mattered, especially those she had felt under-estimated her. She had hired a caterer (also from Piet's stable) to do all the cooking and serving. Her domestic worker had a new suit, and the garden boy looked like a prisoner in his brand-new orange overalls. "You must keep the house neat even when the visitors are here," she told them. "I don't want to see spilled wine or empty glasses or dirt in the garden."

The garden was immaculate, as was the large swimming pool, which was at the foot of the small hill next to the house. The palm leaves in the garden were shining as if someone had put Vaseline on them. Piet's wife brought flowers, glasses, plates and tablecloths, which she arranged prettily throughout the vast living area.

Some of the rooms in the house were furnished in such a way that there was not a trace of personality in them, while others brought to mind an overly made-up face. Lebo's huge bedroom had several doors opening onto a Jacuzzi, steam room, study, gym and a walk-in wardrobe. The furniture was designed and made according to her specifications—dark wood with silver trimmings. The bed was big and round, with Egyptian cotton bedding. Yet Lebo preferred sleeping on the floor most days.

The guests were arriving when Piet and his son came in with the alcohol. He had bought only the most expensive stuff—Johnny Walker Blue Label, Moët—and boxes of it. Even though Lebo ate only traditional food and didn't drink, she made sure that her guests were given the finest fare. She was the kind of person who ate pap and meat for breakfast directly from the pot, and cornflakes in the evening in a salad bowl, but on this occasion she instructed the caterer to arrange serving points and tables inside and outside the house.

On arrival guests were welcomed on the patio with glasses of sherry or champagne and plates of hors d'oeuvres. Everyone was surprised and impressed that it seemed to be white people managing the party. Even though some guests made sarcastic remarks or smiled condescendingly, most of them were generous with their praise. *I will show them! They think they are educated. I will teach them a thing or two,* Lebo said to herself.

Although the educated intimidated Lebo, she believed that proximity to them made her cleverer. There were doctors, lawyers, engineers, politicians, you name it. Almost a hundred and fifty people filled her house and yard. They were in the pool house, in the gazebos, the balconies and verandas with their potted palms and ferns.

Piet and his sons helped to grill the meat outside. The boys tried hard to hide their disdain. They knew that showing their resentment would be biting the hand that fed them.

Most of the guests were shocked to be cooked for by white people, and were even more taken aback when, later, Piet took some of Lebo's relatives to spend the night in his guest house.

"Lebo, the *inyanga* that you consult with is strong—otherwise there is no way that a white man could be this kind to blacks, allowing them to sleep in his blankets. I don't think you consulted a South African *inyanga*, they can't do this. It had to be a Mozambican or a Zimbabwean," said Lebo's step-father.

"I worked for white people for many years. I know them well. They never behave like this."

"Papa, don't say such things. My pastor is here. I pray. I don't do *inyangas*," Lebo whispered in his ear.

Lebo had invited a few people from her village—her relatives and her teacher. She walked in and out of the house wearing a satisfied expression. Her mission to please and impress was accomplished.

It was a clear summer's day and the sun spilled its yellow light through the big wooden window frames and balconies into the rooms. Lebo hoped this light would enter her guests' hearts too. "Did you see their faces? No one will ever undermine me again," she said to her domestic worker.

Lebo's learned friends curbed their sophisticated cynicism and resentment until they were drunk from the whiskey and wine. They had taken over the upstairs living room, which had a bar and a spacious balcony. Anyone who was not in their league would not last two minutes in there. Most of them had no tolerance for cerebral lightweights—apart from Lebo, who was an exception to that rule. If you were not educated, you could get a headache from listening to them throwing big English words around as if the language belonged to them.

Although most of the guests were mesmerized by their surroundings, these erudite friends were less easily impressed.

"*Yaa*! Although it might be considered stylish to be served by whites, it does not feel sensible," said Ntombi, a businesswoman and socialite.

"I agree. She could have given the business to her fellow blacks who really need jobs," said Joe Zulu, a manager at the Eastgate Mall, who was known for his fondness for radical rhetoric. One would have expected him to be on Lebo's side, as he and his family had been staying in Lebo's townhouse for five months, and had yet to pay a cent for rent. Lebo came in when the topic of houses featured in *Top Billing* cropped up. Ntombi highlighted that taste was important when you decorated a house. She pointed out that some people naturally did not have taste.

"Who needs taste when you can pay someone to decorate for you? If you have money, you will have taste. After all, taste without money is useless," said Lebo.

"Lebo, I like your furniture. But you just need to add a little color. The beige and brown are too dull for me," said Ntombi.

"Then it's a good thing you don't live here. You can do color in your own house," said Lebo.

"You know what? Color is good. It brings warmth into the room. Put in a little orange, lime, or turquoise and you'll see what a difference it makes," Ntombi insisted.

Lebo felt a leadenness in her chest. She decided to ignore her, but Ntombi persisted. The others could tell that she was crossing a line but did not attempt to rescue her.

"Do you ever watch *Top Billing*? If you watch it, you will understand what I mean. You should also get hold of some magazines like *House and Leisure* and *Garden and Home*," said Ntombi.

"Look, Ntombi, I invited you here to celebrate with me. Not to critique my decor," said Lebo.

"No, Lebo, don't take it badly. We would not be good friends if we didn't offer good advice," said Ntombi in the same tone Lebo used with people in the village.

Lebo knew and understood that tone very well, and it enraged her.

"Ntombi, I'm afraid I am going to have to ask you to leave. I was under the impression I was among friends here, and I don't think you are one of them. And please don't forget about the money you owe me. I want it by month's end." More than half of the people in the room owed Lebo something, and she looked at them with special intent.

Despite trying to rally support, Ntombi was renounced. People changed the topic and pretended she was not there, but still she stood firm, refusing to leave.

Ten minutes later, Lebo's step-father and step-uncle approached Ntombi. "Sesi! I think it would be best if you left now peacefully, before we show you how we deal with jealous people like you in our village," said Lebo's uncle.

The others continued with their conversations as if nothing was happening. Ntombi reached for her bag and left without any goodbyes. Passing Lebo, she made a last attempt to make amends.

"Lebo, I am sorry," she said.

"Sesi, don't waste our time. Just get out," said Lebo's domestic worker on her behalf.

"Hey, you *straatmeisie*, I am talking to Lebo, not you," said Ntombi.

"Ntombi, I don't want to talk to a piece of rubbish like you. You heard her, get out," said Lebo.

The domestic worker and Lebo pushed her outside. "You call me rubbish, but the real rubbish is you! I don't sleep with white people to get rich. Look at you, you are just a white man's slave. Nothing more!" Ntombi shouted.

The security guards were now carrying her like a seventy-kilogram bag of mealie-meal. They threw her outside the gate where her car was parked. Everyone was watching the drama from the balconies and patios.

"Lebo! You will pay for this. You illiterate bitch!" she howled.

Ntombi was not the kind of person who took things lying down. She was well connected in Nelspruit and she did all she could to drag Lebo's name into the sewer. She had taken pictures during the party and she immediately forwarded these to a journalist working for *The Lowvelder*.

She released information about Lebo fronting for white men who were making a fortune that they didn't deserve.

Even after hosting a party that cost fifty thousand rand, Lebo still felt insecure. The next Tuesday she received an early-morning call from one of her friends telling her to get a copy of *The Lowvelder*. She felt sick when she read the article, knowing it was Ntombi's doing. Without delay, she went to her *inyanga*, whom she instructed to make Ntombi go insane. The *inyanga* gave Lebo an ash-like concoction to spread in Ntombi's yard.

That afternoon, Lebo decided to go and see her grandmother. On the way there, she checked on a friend she used to work with at the lawyers' office.

"Lebo, I am happy you came. A woman called Ntombi came here asking questions about you," said Lebo's friend.

"She is crazy, that one. She is trying to destroy me."

Her friend told her that Ntombi had been spreading rumors about her in the village.

"She goes about telling people that *wena*, you are having an affair with an old white man. She said that all the things you claim are yours belong to the white man. She has told people that you use your buttocks to get rich."

When Lebo left the surgery, she cried bitterly in the car. She could not understand why her own people were not happy about her success. When she told her grandmother what Ntombi had said, the old lady replied, "They must leave you alone, my child. No one is stopping them from using their own buttocks. If their buttocks can't work for them, it is not your fault."

Lebo prayed that night. She realized what a huge effort it was to keep everyone impressed. She also realized that the civilized world was not as perfect as it seemed on the surface. It was narrow, stifling, and full of petty prejudice. She now started dreaming new dreams. Her latest desire was to go back to school, to become an engineer. She knew Piet would help her. She daydreamed and saw herself in a white lab coat at Wits University.

Months later, when she had forgotten about their feud, a friend told her that Ntombi had been admitted to Weskoppies Psychiatric Hospital.

She wondered what had really worked—her prayers or the *inyanga's* concoction. Either way, it didn't make her feel any happier. She still had the sense that there was something missing, that there would always be something missing.

For a time, the door to her dream-world stood ajar, until one day it closed forever.

Vicious Cycle

I'm not sure why I agreed when Adichie invited me to go for a picnic with him and his Norwegian friend. The combination of Adichie, a Nigerian PhD student at Rhodes, and Peter, a professor in the Sociology Department, was usually more than I could bear at a time. It was impossible for those two to snap out of academic mode.

It was a clear November Sunday, with the sun casting its full warm rays on our seats. Adichie and Peter sat in the front of the car while I sat in the back with Peter's two children.

I was quiet for most of the trip. My silence made them uncomfortable because they knew me to be chatty.

"Are you OK?" asked Adichie.

"I'm fine. Don't mind me. I'm just a bit tired," I said. The truth was that I was intimidated by the two academics' seriousness and lack of humor. I was not in the mood to fight intellectual wars. Nor did I want to be made to feel embarrassed by my ignorance. So I left them to eloquently contest one another from different points of view, even on topics they agreed on.

Since I had come to Rhodes University, I'd learned to avoid academics as far as possible when I wanted to enjoy myself and unwind. I found it hard to relax while discussing theories and philosophies. I preferred uninhibited, simple conversations and would rather leave the theories for the lecture halls. I had just submitted my final essay and my head was still rattling as if there were tins and nails in it. My brain needed a break. I would have preferred to go and unwind in the township.

I sat there with the five-year-old twins, a girl and a boy.

Their father kept on checking them in the rearview mirror and talking to them in Norwegian. They were born in South Africa and had only visited Norway during holidays. Peter bragged to us about how he had single-handedly taught them his home language. Every now and then he paused from his clever talk with Adichie to say something to the children.

I found myself envying the twins. I wished I could go back to my childhood and have a father that was this attentive. Or that I return to my youth and re-conceive my two boys with a man this caring. I later discovered that Peter was separated from his Xhosa wife and his children were now living with him full time. I wondered about what could have caused the split. *If I had a man who cared about children this much, I would never leave him*, I thought.

I became lost in my thoughts, as the two men engaged in their intellectual gymnastics. As we drove through the green mountains that separated Grahamstown and the nature reserve, I began to explore the darker tracks of my life. There was a bitter taste in my mouth as my thoughts turned to my father and my children's father.

I recalled how, when he was fifteen, my younger son, Gamza, ran away from home to look for his father. He hitch-hiked to Thohoyandou town, where Luvhengo, his father, lived. He went straight to the police station where Luvhengo worked and asked for him. He did not even know what his father looked like, as the last time he had seen him was when he was a year old. They told him that he was on leave and would be back in two days' time. My son did not push to find out where his father's home was, as he was afraid that Luvhengo's new wife might not like him. He roamed around the town for two days, sleeping in the graveyard at night. In the meantime, I was looking for him everywhere, and I had filed a missing person's case in Polokwane, where we lived.

On the third day, my son met his father for the first time. Gamza said he was amazed by how much he looked like him. Luvhengo took my son to KFC and bought him a Streetwise Two.

They sat and he ate. The boy said he was happy to have met him and had all kinds of hopes for their newfound relationship.

"I want to come and stay with you," my son told his father. "I am tired of my mother's husband calling us luckless and fatherless bastards." Gamza told his father everything, including the fact that my current husband was abusive and not contributing much financially in our home, which belonged to me.

Apparently Luvhengo listened attentively, remaining silent for some time. When it was his turn to respond, he said, "Look, son, I am happy that you have hunted me down. It is a good thing that we now know each other. You see, life is more complicated than you think. I am a clerk at the police station. I earn very little. I am not as rich as your mother, who is educated.

"Look at you: you are wearing clothes that I cannot afford, even for myself. Nike shoes, a Puma T-shirt ... I know how much those things cost. You probably go to a private school. What I am telling you is that as much as I might want you to live with me, I could never afford to look after you. I have another wife with five children. Our house has two bedrooms, you see.

"Another thing is that my wife fought a lot with your mother years ago. I don't think she will accept you. I am sorry, but you have to go back to your mother. Life with her is much better than what I can offer."

Luvhengo then told Gamza to give him my number, and took out his cellphone from his jacket. I remember how surprised I was to receive a call from him.

"Hello, Mapula. It's me, Luvhengo. I am with Gamza here. He said he hitchhiked—"

"What? Where?" I interrupted him. He then ran out of airtime and I had to call him back.

"You must come and fetch him. I told him you are a good mother," said Luvhengo.

I was so annoyed with him for rejecting my son like that. But I wasn't shocked, because he had never cared enough to contribute a cent towards bringing up the two boys. I hadn't even bothered to take him to the maintenance court.

I told Gamza to meet me at the Caltex garage. I warned him not to bring his father along as I might kill him. He couldn't even make a plan to get his son back home. In the car, Gamza was mute. I did not say anything either. I could see the hurt in his black eyes. I left him alone with his thoughts and focused on my own anger.

It was overcast that day. Large silver clouds drifted slowly across the sky, now and then obscuring the sun. I hated cloudy days. It was a grey-sky day when Luvhengo left me with two kids for a younger woman. And it was hazy the day my recent husband first hit me and called my sons bastards.

A few days later, when the anger had subsided, I appreciated the fact that at least Luvhengo had been upfront with my son. I recalled the incident of Mumsy's son, who also went looking for his father. The boy found out that his father was in fact a well-to-do someone—or rather he gave the boy that impression. He promised the boy all sorts of things—a PlayStation, a bicycle, new clothes, and to take him out of government school so that he could go to a private school like his step-brother.

Mumsy warned her son not to get too excited as his father was the most unreliable person she had ever known. But the boy chose to believe him. They had set a date on which they were going to meet to buy all these things. The man did not pitch, nor bother to postpone. From that day on, he avoided the boy's calls. When Mumsy's son used a public phone, he dropped the phone as soon as he heard the young boy's voice. One late afternoon on a Tuesday, Mumsy came home from work, tired. She opened the garage door to park her car, only to find her worst nightmare. Her son was hanging from the garage ceiling.

I talked to my son and told him that it was not the end of the world. I assured him that his father's rejection did not define who he was, and that it wasn't his fault. It would only affect him if he allowed it to. I said that there were many great men who had grown up with absent fathers. I told him the story of Walter

Sisulu. Sisulu's father, a white man who employed his mother as a domestic worker, died denying that he was his father. And look at how successful he became. He was now a world-known icon who had fought for South African democracy.

Gamza's face lit up, and he said, "Mom, don't worry. I am fine. I understand."

I was relieved. "Now don't go and do anything stupid—like committing suicide without discussing it with me first," I said, and he laughed.

A month after that incident, my new husband asked me for money to install a music system in the car that I had bought for him. When I refused, he shouted at me, calling me a selfish bitch. He told me that he had done me a favor by marrying me, with my two bastards, as no other man would have done. He was shouting so loudly that I was sure my sons could hear him. I decided to shut myself in my office and catch up on some work, to distract myself from my angry thoughts.

That day my two sons, 15- and 17-years-old, decided it was time to discipline my husband. They knew he hated loud music and played it anyway. When he came downstairs, he screamed at them as usual, telling them that they should go and live with their father because they were disturbing his peace. Normally my sons would have kept quiet and lowered the volume.

"If you want your peace, why don't you go and buy yourself a house? Like a normal man. This is our home. You found us staying here. You must adapt to our ways or go to wherever you came here from."

"If it was up to us, you would not be living in this house. We are just putting up with you because we have no choice," said my older son, Rudzani.

"What?" my husband responded.

"We are sick and tired of your verbal abuse. Go and feel sorry for yourself in your own house and abuse your own children, if you have any," the boy added.

"Just who do you think you're talking to?" my husband

raged. "How dare you! You don't know me. I will ..." He tried to punch Rudzani, but Gamza came from behind and hit him with his cricket bat. The boys were stronger than my husband had imagined. At that moment they attacked him jointly, overpowering him. Side tables and vases were knocked over as he stumbled out of the room and headed upstairs. He burst into my office, where I had been listening to the altercation, hoping to avoid having to get involved.

"I can't live with those savages anymore. I am going. You can call me when they are no longer there. Maybe I will still be available," he said.

"What do you want me to do? Kill them? They are my children. You are the one who has turned them into monsters. They learned violence from you," I said.

"Then you must sleep with them. I am going," he said.

"Where will you go?" I asked.

"Don't ask me questions," he said.

"OK," I said quietly.

I was tired of him treating me like I should be grateful to have him. I was drained by his abuse, his irresponsibility, and sense of entitlement. Fortunately, we were married out of community of property. The wisest decision I ever took with regard to him. I'd insisted on it despite his efforts at dissuasion, as I had a lot more to lose.

After leaving, he did not call and nor did I. I realized how much happier my sons were without him in the house. I felt bad for having put them through a fatherless childhood and then imposing a useless husband on them. I decided it was time for a new start: a divorce and a change of career. That is how I ended up back at Rhodes University. I enrolled my sons at St Andrew's College in Grahamstown. It was one of the best schools in the country. The small university town was a different world from Limpopo, where people were defined by their marital status.

"A penny for your thoughts," said Adichie from the front seat.

"Oh, I was just daydreaming," I said.

The reserve was beautiful. At the gate, there was a viewpoint from which one could see the river circling the mountains like a necklace. I now understood why it was called Water's Meeting.

The reflection of the trees made the river-water green. I could have stood there for hours, taking it all in. We drove down a rocky gravel road to the river. There was a picnic spot with wooden tables and benches and a braai area. Peter helped the twins change into their swimming costumes. He then gave them their *padkos*—biscuits, juice, and apples. In my world, men who did what he did for his children were as scarce as Indian policemen in Polokwane.

The river water was clear. Peter jumped in and floated with the girl on his back, holding the boy in front. It was a perfect picture of fatherhood. I watched them while sitting on the concrete bridge-like structure that crossed the river, with my feet in the water. I couldn't believe I was jealous of five-year-olds. I tried to entertain myself by counting tadpoles in the water. I stirred them with a stick and was amused when they swam in different directions. Adichie sat within talking distance of me, reading the *City Press* newspaper.

"Is he sure this water is safe? Are we sure they don't have crocodiles here?" said Adichie, and I laughed.

"They would have written a warning if there were," I said.

Adichie was a short, middle-aged man who always overemphasized what he said, as if you wouldn't believe him otherwise. Everyone acquainted with Adichie knew that he couldn't have a conversation with any South African without comparing their country to Nigeria. With him, it was always, "In Nigeria, we don't do this" or "In Nigeria, we do things like that." He would always mention that he had been an associate professor at a Nigerian university but had done his other PhD in the USA. When I first met him, I thought he was strange. But by now I had grown used to him, and had stopped judging him.

My phone rang and it was my mother. Since I left Limpopo, we'd speak on the phone a few times every week. I stood up and walked across the bridge, trying to find better reception. Adichie went back to his paper.

"It must be a boyfriend you were talking to for so long," said Adichie.

I laughed. "No, it was my mom. Updating me on the latest from back home," I told him.

"You know I've noticed that you black South Africans always talk about your mothers. But never your fathers. Why is that?"

I felt like he was reading my mind. I tried to turn the conversation back to him, teasing. "Adichie, I think the second PhD is driving you mad. Too much reading is not good for you," I said.

I knew what was coming. This was a sensitive topic for me. I feared conversations about fathers the way other people feared dentists. I knew that men lacked the sensitivity to speak the truth with care. I had also become aware that most of those who grew up with fathers were painfully unsympathetic and insensitive to those who hadn't. That is because they didn't know how it felt. A man who was pursuing me once said on our first date that most people who were not raised by their fathers were abnormal. "They always have some kind of issues," he said. I didn't dispute his theory.

I was not ready to venture into this topic with Adichie. But he persisted.

"You know what I am talking about: most men here abandon their children. In Nigeria, that never happens at all."

"Really?" I said.

"Yes. It is an embarrassing situation. Do you know a bird does better than most South African black men when it comes to looking after its youth? And it doesn't even have a job," he said.

I forced a laugh and saw him examining my face.

"You know this thing started when people were migrant workers, coming home twice a year. Those boys who grew up under those conditions were never taught by anyone how to be a father. Fatherhood is a learned behavior," said Adichie.

He was right. I could think of very little evidence of enchanting father-and-child relationships among black families in South Africa.

After a long walk in the forest, we were finally back in the car and on our way home. Adichie and I did not enjoy the walk as much as Peter and his twins, who loved hiking. Adichie kept on hinting that it might not be safe, as lions and leopards could have crossed from the local game farms to look for food.

Sitting back, I left the two men to resume their conversation. This time Adichie was defending Africa. "Africa is the butt of every international joke. You Europeans should leave us to live our own lives the way we know best," said Adichie.

"You say Africa this, Africa that, and yet there would never have been an Africa if we hadn't come and discovered it and even named it for you," said Peter.

I was amused by the way Adichie was not offended by this statement.

As the two men continued throwing word missiles at each other, my thoughts returned to the men in my life. I recalled the day, five years back, when I met my dad for the first time. I had accepted that he was not part of our life and I did not think much about him. It is difficult to miss a stranger. I felt some sense of loss over not having a biological father, but not over him. My step-father had raised us well. But for my brother, this was not enough. He was obsessed with meeting his real father.

That day, I drove my mother and brother to a place called Mtititi, on a mission to find our father. The village was in the middle of a dense forest, near the Kruger National Park. We drove through the heat on the rough gravel road, finally arriving in the late afternoon. The first building we came across in Mtititi was a small, flat-roofed school, beyond which was a cluster of *rondawels*. We soon got lost: it had been many years since my mother had left the village. The women we stopped to ask for directions took a quarter of an hour greeting us. They laid out their whole lineage to us, as if it were the most important thing in the world, and they were eager to share tidbits of village gossip.

The mud huts gave the rural settlement an ashen look. The August winds were wild and dust from the dry earth spread everywhere. Everyone's face was made up with a brown mascara of dust.

"Your father did me a favor by leaving me. Imagine! I would still be stuck in this place, rotting like an overripe tomato," said my mother. "I would have never studied to become a teacher. You, Tshepo, would be minding some chief's cattle for no salary. Look at this place, there is nothing. Where would one get a job here? It's far from everything."

My father, who had worked in Johannesburg most of his life, was now back in his home village. Shortly after I was born, he had abandoned my mother and us and gone back to Johannesburg. After several years, when he did not return, my mother packed her belongings (including us) and left.

Finally, we arrived at my father's home. The yard was big, like most rural yards, and they had planted corn in the back. I saw three goats tied with a long rope to some trees towards the left of the plot.

A small, windowless thatched hut stood in the center of the yard. A dirty cloth served as a door. A short adult would have to bend to enter the hut. Then there was a small square house built recklessly from grey block bricks.

Its windows had no glass; instead, a sheet of corrugated iron covered the window spaces.

A thin woman wearing an oversized brown dress with a matching pinafore met us at the small gate. "It must be the wife," whispered my mother as she approached and directed us into the grey house. Walking close to her, I caught the scent of baked earth coming from her emaciated body. Inside, the air was stifling. Harsh coughing sounds could be heard from another room. There was a wooden bench and a small table in the corner, around which were a few white garden chairs. Plastic crates pushed beneath the table served as cabinets. The linoleum-tiled floor was sticky with grime and dust. My mother looked at me and shook her head. "Please, can we rather sit outside in the shade? The heat in this house is making my blood pressure rise," she said.

After a while, a man came outside and walked slowly towards us. He wore a pair of old, torn jeans and a shirt that was frayed at its hems. His complexion was dark, but the undersides of his arms were lighter in tone. He had an odd way of walking, as if he were being pushed from behind by a gust of wind. The sun was now concealed by patches of dark cloud. It seemed like it was going to rain.

So this is my father, I thought. I was not impressed. The whole thing did not feel real. I felt like I was in a movie. It was obvious that my brother felt differently. He stood up from the bench and remained standing until the older man sat down next to him. My brother's eyes were filled with tears. I wondered if these were tears of joy or something else. His life was in chaos. He had been fired from his job at Ackermans because of drunkenness. I was now supporting him and his family financially.

I felt nothing for my father. I decided the whole venture was a complete waste of time. I was only interested in how much the man looked like my brother.

"Mokope, how are you?" the man said to my mother. His smile exposed his missing front teeth. His eyes were dull and the lids heavy, so that he looked as if he were about to fall asleep.

"I am fine, I have brought your children," she said. I could not understand why she did not seem to be angry with him. Maybe it was because she had moved on, got married, and found happiness with my step-father.

He stood up and shook our hands. His hand was rough against my palm. I hated myself for being so unmoved, but I just could not help it. *From his wrecked appearance, it looks like he has paid for even his future sins*, I thought.

"You are all grown up. The last time I saw you, you were just babies," the man said.

We just looked at him and kept quiet. I wanted to ask him why he had not come to see us in all those years. *But it was pointless,* I thought. *It wouldn't change anything.* My eyes moved to the goats that were grazing. I could not understand why they had to be tied to the trees. I wondered how I would have felt if I was one of them. *Maybe I am a goat,* I thought. *I am also tied to men who couldn't care less about me.*

"They are both working now," my mother was answering for us. "Mapula works for the government. They now have their own children." My mother was one of those people that never mentioned her children's failures to anyone. She did not say a word about my brother's dismissal from work. She viewed us as an extension of herself, and our misfortunes became hers too. When I went through a divorce, it was as if it were my mother's marriage that was ending, not mine. Sometimes I felt like her pain was worse than mine.

"Mhh! A government job! That is good. My girl, maybe you can buy your old daddy a small van so that I can sell tomatoes in the village. I have a license. I was a truck driver in Joburg."

Something snapped in me and I started hustling them to leave.

"I have work to do in the office," I said. I regretted the whole exercise. It had been futile. I was even more irritated when my brother hugged him.

The memories of my father still chafed as the car drove into Grahamstown. Peter dropped Adichie and me at the Spur. Adichie had offered to buy me supper.

"You are very quiet," Adichie said while we were waiting for our steaks.

"I was just thinking about what you said," I told him.

"We can't blame these men for not being involved with their children," said Adichie.

"Why?"

"Because, like I said earlier, love is a learned thing. It is through the love of a father that you learn how to be a father. Their fathers were never there—they were working in Johannesburg in the mines. So this thing has become a vicious cycle," he said.

"Well, someone should break it. Things can't continue like this. Men don't seem to feel the slightest guilt about the children they've fathered and then abandoned. It is the most normal and acceptable thing in black communities. I respect the white brothers for seeing things differently," I said.

"I don't know. You are the writer. Maybe you can create awareness and make people start debating solutions. But if you South Africans don't do anything, you will end up with a very angry youth. The signs are already there. Take for instance this ANC Youth League president Julius Malema. I don't think he was raised with a father present."

I was chewing my steak when he said that. It tasted like a face-cloth. I struggled to swallow, but eventually it went down. I looked at Adichie and faked a smile again.

"You know what? I am going to get a doggy bag. I will eat this later. Thank you so much," I said.

I felt my anger subsiding. An urge to forgive my father suddenly came over me, and for the first time that I could remember, I was able to feel pity for him. Leaving the Spur that evening, I felt hopeful that one day all my hatred would fade, maybe even vanish like clouds when the sun comes out.

The Things We Do For Love

Ngwato came home at midnight that Friday. He was drunk and struggled to drive his BMW up the steep driveway. He decided to push the accelerator down all the way so that the car would maintain power up the hill. When he reached the top of the driveway, his foot was still on the accelerator. The car smashed through the garage door into the two cars that were parked there, pushing the Volkswagen Passat through the wall that separated the garage and the kitchen. When his BMW came to a standstill, he climbed out and walked towards the front door. By the time he reached the veranda, he thought it was his bedroom. He took off his clothes and lay down on the floor in his underwear.

Mosima woke with a start, but assumed that it must be her husband arriving home. His coming home late was no longer an issue. It was something she was used to. She turned over and went back to sleep. He had his own key and his food was in the oven if he was hungry.

A loud banging sound woke her up again. It sounded like the house was being demolished.

An earthquake? No, it can't be, she thought. She could hear movements, which meant her children were also up. She jumped out of bed and grabbed her nightgown and cellphone.

She found her three boys standing in the passage. Molebatsi, the oldest at fourteen, was holding his cricket bat.

"Mom, what was that sound?" he asked.

"Go into your room. It's nothing, don't panic," she said, trying hard to hide her own fear.

"Where is Papa?" said the youngest, who was eight.

"I'll be back now-now," she said, closing the door and heading for the stairs. Her cellphone rang. It was their driver, Moses, phoning from the servants' quarters at the back.

"It's Molebatsi's father—he has smashed the garage. Come down."

She ran fast down the stairs, almost stumbling after missing a step. Downstairs she found the Volkswagen in the kitchen. Bricks and chunks of cement were everywhere. Her glass-top stove was in pieces.

"Mhhh!" she said quietly. She ran through the living area and saw Moses through the glass front door outside, pointing at something.

She opened the door to find her husband lying in his briefs. His clothes were piled on the cane sofa.

"Is he dead? What is wrong?" she asked, with her hand on her mouth.

"I found him here. I don't think he is dead. He is breathing. I think he is drunk," said the driver.

She cried out loud, "*Yoo nna mmawe*! Who took his clothes off?"

"I don't know. I found him like this."

He was now snoring loudly, clearly not dead.

"I am going to check on the boys. Carry him into the guest room."

The guest room was downstairs. She did not want the children to see him like this. She put the boys back to sleep, assuring them that all was well. Moses was still waiting for her in the living room when she returned.

"Moses, I am calling the police. Maybe people were chasing him," Mosima said.

"No ma'am. I think you should wait for him to wake up. If you are afraid, I will stay here and guard the place, but we can't call the police when he is still this drunk."

"It's fine, go back to sleep. I will call you if something happens."

Mosima was a woman with quiet strength. There was a

dignity about her, even under these circumstances. She walked outside with Moses and stopped at the garage to assess the damage. She decided to call Phuti, Ngwato's cousin, the only person who was not afraid of him. Everyone around Ngwato depended on him financially. No one else, including his mother, was brave enough to tell him when he was at fault.

"I think your cousin is bewitched. He drove into the house and we found him naked on the veranda. I am telling you, his girlfriends are bewitching him. They want me to leave," Mosima said, crying.

"He was just drunk. Don't frustrate yourself with that cheap psychology. Just thank God he was not harmed. As for the property, that you can always replace," Phuti said.

"He needs help. This cannot be normal."

"Get some sleep. I will come over and talk to him tomorrow," Phuti said.

The following afternoon, Phuti came to check on them. Ngwato sat there on the veranda step, a glass of iced water next to him. His face was hidden between his legs. He did not raise it when Phuti sat down next to him.

"I knew you were coming. I knew she had called you. Maybe I should put you on my employee's payroll: the family social worker," he said, with his face still covered.

Phuti said nothing and sat there admiring the garden and the view of Duiwelskloof dam down in the valley. *How can people that are living in heaven, here on earth, be this unhappy?* she thought.

Ngwato raised his head and looked at Phuti with blood-shot eyes.

"I hope you are not coming here to preach to me. I'm going to tell you exactly what I told Mosima. This is my problem, and no one else's."

Phuti still did not say anything. She looked at him, shook her head, and smiled. Then she moved her eyes back to the scenic contours of the mountains in the distance. She behaved as though she had not heard what he'd said.

Mosima came out the front door. Her eyes were red from crying. She had been crying when she called Phuti around mid-night, and was still crying when Phuti called her in the morning, and she must have been crying just before she came out onto the veranda.

"Can I use your car to fetch the children from school? You know our cars ..." she said.

"*Yaa* sure," Phuti replied, handing her the keys to her car.

"Why don't you call Moses?" said Ngwato. "He can fetch them in the Navara. I am not comfortable with my kids driving in that old scrap."

Mosima stopped, startled, but ignored him and started the Nissan van, which was not a scrap at all. Phuti knew that he wanted to make his wife angry to divert her attention from the issue at hand.

"Look, you know what? My accident is my personal issue. I will deal with it in my own time, in my own way. I am not a small boy. I don't like being reprimanded," he said.

Phuti said nothing. This time she did not even look at him.

"*Bona!* Yes, last night I came home drunk, in my BMW, hit my garage door and wall, and again I hit my Audi Q7, which hit my Passat and broke my kitchen wall. These are my things ... my cars ... my house. I worked hard for them. I don't understand how you or Mosima can have anything to do with it." There was a deep silence before he added, "I want you to understand me clearly. I didn't kill anybody or harm anything that belongs to anyone else. It's my problem and I know how to solve it."

Phuti burst into laughter.

"That idiot wife of mine wanted to call the police. What does she know? She does not even know how much all these things cost me," he said.

"Tell me, what did you smoke last night?" Phuti asked him.

"What do you mean? I was just drunk."

"It can't be just alcohol. Whatever it is, it's still in your system. I can tell from the things you are saying." Phuti paused and looked into his eyes for a second. "You are definitely not yourself. Whatever it is you have taken, ditch it and try something else, because it really doesn't work for you."

He kept quiet.

"You seem to forget that you are no longer a naughty village boy who can get away with anything. You are a public figure and you need to protect your image. Or else you can kiss that job of yours goodbye. Where have you seen a minister of Public Works behaving like this?" she said.

"Don't patronize me. You know I don't do any drugs."

"I am not trying to patronize you. Not that I care if I am. The only thing I care about is that you should apologize to that poor wife of yours who made the stupid decision to stay with a mad person like you for the rest of her life. She is a nice girl. She does not need this rubbish," she said.

"You know I don't take drugs," Ngwato repeated.

"And you know I am not only talking about the drugs. You are frustrating that sweet girl who is trying so hard to keep a decent home for you."

"Does she pay you to say such nice things about her? You don't know her. Anyway, just don't forget who your real relative is—me, not her."

That sat in silence for a while, each lost in thought, until Mosima returned in the Nissan. Phuti greeted the three boys and said her goodbyes. She noticed that their faces were a bit gloomy.

When she reversed, she heard Ngwato saying to Mosima, "She thinks she is Margaret Thatcher. She will never get married if she keeps bullying everyone the way she does. Who does she think she is? She knows nothing about marriage."

Phuti knew this to be an attempt to appease his wife.

She returned the next day, and this time Ngwato was more repentant.

"*Eish,*" he lamented, before she said anything, "I have burnt the eggs, big time. She is not talking to me. Every time she looks at me, she cries. Tell me, how can I make things right? Maybe I must buy her a new car—a Mercedes. I know she loves them," he said.

"What happened?" Phuti asked.

"My last memory was being at Peter Mawasha's place, holding a glass of Johnny Walker Blue. The rest I can't tell you. I don't even recall driving home," he said.

"You need to apologize to her. If alcohol has that kind of effect on you, give it up. You will drive her mad. You need to get your act together. This lifestyle of yours, with your girlfriends and parties, is just not on for a politician like you. It is disgusting. You live like a character out of a Chinua Achebe novel. If you are not careful, these people will eat you alive. Politics is a dirty game. You are all over the place. And *yaa*! What is this that I hear, that you go everywhere with that *skheberesh* who works at the municipality? I heard she was also in Durban when you took your family for a holiday," Phuti said.

"Since when did you become a gossip-monger? Where do you get these stupid stories?"

"They are not rumors. That girl goes around boasting to everyone about it. What is a person with such a high portfolio doing with that thing? If you really have to cheat, couldn't you do it with someone more respectable? Like those ladies from parliament, they can be discreet. And save your wife the humiliation that this stupid girl is putting her through."

"You are judging me because you know nothing. At least I have only one girlfriend—most of those guys in Cabinet have several. The president has four wives and a girlfriend in every province. No, not province, in every town. It is African culture. This is how our grandfathers used to live."

"Yes, but in your grandfather's time there was no HIV."

She saw no point in pursuing the topic. It was too depressing for her. She felt sorry for his wife who was at that time attending a meeting at the children's school. Even though she lived in lavish comfort, Phuti did not envy Mosima. She knew she could not survive in such a marriage.

"I have to go. I have an appointment with someone," she said to Ngwato.

"If it's a potential husband, tell him I said he must hurry up and marry you. You are not getting any younger."

"After the crap that you have just told me, I think I would prefer to stay single. I will marry in my next life, when I am a pigeon or a locust."

Later that day Phuti could not keep Ngwato's words out of her mind. She thought about Mosima and all she was going through. Was it ever going to end?

Indeed, Ngwato seemed to feel no remorse about his infidelity. He had sneaked his girlfriend into the hotel in Durban, where he was staying with his wife and children. She was in a room on the floor beneath theirs. Every morning he would dispatch the family with Moses to go shopping, sightseeing, and swimming while he nestled for hours with his girlfriend drinking whiskey and smoking pot.

"I like the fact that when I am with you I can be myself," he told his girlfriend.

He had told Mosima that he was having meetings with KwaZulu-Natal politicians.

"You work too hard," she said. "You need a break too, you know."

"I have to work hard for us to be able to afford places like this," Ngwato replied.

Every morning at breakfast, Mosima saw a young woman sitting alone. It was not hard to notice her because she was the only other black person in the hotel restaurant. She was attractive, with large eyes and straight, shiny black hair combed into a wave that curled around her neck.

On the third morning, Mosima greeted her while they were waiting for omelets at the buffet. She asked the young woman where she was from.

"Joburg," she said.

"Are you here on business or vacation?" Mosima asked in a kind tone.

"Business," the young woman answered, with her eyes focused on the chef who was busy frying the omelets. Mosima had wanted to ask her what type of business but was discouraged by the woman's brisk answer. Instead she asked her to join her family's table. The woman refused politely, saying she had to rush off somewhere. She did not strike Mosima as the business type.

"Maybe tomorrow," said the woman with a half-smile.

Ngwato watched them anxiously from the table, wondering what in the world they could be talking about. Mosima admired how young and fresh the woman looked. The girl reminded her a little of herself in her heyday, before she'd married Ngwato.

"Who is that woman? Do you know her?" asked Ngwato.

"*Eish*, that poor woman, she is always alone at breakfast. I invited her to join us and she said maybe tomorrow," said Mosima.

"You must be careful with strangers. This is not Limpopo. You can't go around trusting people you don't know. She could be a journalist or a spy. You need to be discreet. You are a big man's wife," he said and then buried himself in his newspaper. He almost laughed at her naivety.

Later, Ngwato and his girlfriend joked about Mosima over a glass of whiskey. "My dear, I see you have married a *modjadji*," she said, cackling with laughter.

Two weeks later, back home, Mosima received a phone call from a male stranger telling her about the Durban girl, Maphefo. The person told her that the girl's fiancé had committed suicide after she left him for Ngwato. He also revealed that Maphefo had been at the same hotel in Durban, on a different floor. At first Mosima did not buy the story, until the image of the girl at breakfast entered her mind. When Mosima discussed the issue with Phuti, she advised her that the person who phoned must have been instructed by Maphefo.

"That stick without a soul," said Mosima.

"It must be a strategy to get you to fight with your husband—maybe even get you out of the picture."

"I will never leave my husband over some cheap *tickiline*. I don't think she loves him. She's only in it for the money," said Mosima.

Phuti could see the fear in Mosima's eyes. She could tell that Mosima was trying to convince herself more than anyone else. She was scared and did not know what to do.

Two months later, Ngwato started staying away from home, making an appearance only every two weeks or so. The male stranger phoned again, telling Mosima he had bought the girl a townhouse in Aquapark suburb, overlooking Tzaneen Dam. After this phone call, Mosima hired someone to investigate. The detective's findings revealed how much Ngwato had spent on the property and furniture.

Phuti advised Mosima to consult a lawyer and get the woman evicted from the house, and then sue her for adultery. Mosima thought about it and decided that it would be a waste of time, as he might buy her another one. Talking to the girl woman-to-woman made more sense. She decided to drive to the complex, where she waited for Maphefo outside. Mosima stopped her as she was driving out. The girl parked her car alongside Mosima's. They stood next to each other, sandwiched by their vehicles.

"I came here to talk to you about my husband. In case you have forgotten, I want to remind you that he is married to me and that he has three boys who are still growing and need him. You can't keep on making him stay away from his home. God will punish you for your cruelty."

"You see, from a woman's point of view, I understand your position. But I think you are talking to the wrong person," Maphefo said.

"What do you mean, you are the wrong person? I know everything," Mosima said, raising her voice.

"The thing is, I can't help you. I love him too. We will have to share him. Otherwise you will have to put a chain on him. You know, like a dog ..."

The girl had not finished her speech before Mosima pushed her against the passenger window of her car. Their heated exchange had become a spectacle. Domestic workers and gardeners stood staring as Mosima kicked the young woman until she fell to the ground. Then she leaped onto her, squatting on top of her so that Maphefo's hands were locked beneath Mosima's feet, and began to hit her in the face. The girl's legs jerked like an epileptic's.

"*Yoo nna mmawe!*" Maphefo screamed.

After several blows to her face, the girl said, "Please stop, you are hurting me. Stop! Please! I will leave Ngwato. I will never see him again."

When the security men at the gate finally separated them, blood was flowing from the girl's nose and mouth, matching her red top.

"If I hear that you are seeing him again, I will kill you. I am not joking," Mosima said, starting her car. From there she went straight to Phuti's house. Phuti was shocked to hear she had fought with the girl. She wanted to tell her that it was the lowest thing to do, but she didn't. As she was leaving Phuti's house, Mosima's domestic worker called and told her that the police were looking for her.

"That stick without a soul had the nerve to call the police. *Sis!*" she spat.

"You know that they will arrest you if they find you. Let me call Ngwato. He created this mess. He must sort it out," Phuti said. She picked up her cellphone.

"Hello, I am with your wife here."

"*Yaa!* I know what happened. How could she be so stupid?"

"She learned from the best—you. Anyway, the Tzaneen police are looking for her. If you don't deal with it, you will be in the headlines of all the newspapers tomorrow."

"I have already done damage control. She has withdrawn the charge," he said.

"Talk to Mosima," Phuti said, but he had hung up.

That night Ngwato did not come home, and the relationship with the girl did not end. It was now an open secret. Maphefo had been elevated to the status of an official deputy wife. Mosima began to feel that she was being punished by God—it was payback for having snatched Ngwato from his fiancé many years before, when they were young. So now the chicken had come back home to roost. Although she realized she should no longer live with him, she knew she would never divorce him. She had made a vow to love him till death. It was an unbearable contradiction.

She buried herself in church activities. This gave her the space to reflect and analyze her position. The few times Ngwato came back home, she treated him like royalty, as if all were well. This irritated him.

A year later the girl was found dead in her apartment. Rumor had it that two unidentified men broke in and shot her in the stomach. Apparently, she had been pregnant. People speculated about who might have killed her, but five years on there was still no evidence and no one had been arrested.

Ngwato discovered that he was being investigated for fraud and had to resign from his post. He was clever enough to see that his political path was strewn with people he'd crossed. He got out before they could crush him completely. For a while, his stories made headlines in all the newspapers.

Following his resignation, the President sent him to Malaysia as an ambassador for South Africa. He took Mosima and the children with him, and life went on.

Take Back the Lobola

I grudgingly drove my mom, a retired teacher, to Marishane for the funeral of her priest's mother. I resented the fact that every time I visited her, I would end up being her unsolicited chauffeur. I had to drive her to funerals, weddings, shops and church, or to visit her bevy of friends.

I cannot deny that at times some of these occasions turned out to be interesting and I ended up enjoying myself. Like last month when I drove her to the wedding of her priest's daughter Makau, who was marrying a gentleman called Mofeti at the Roland Hotel.

Everything was perfect at that wedding, almost too good to be true. The groom told everyone that he had saved enough money to bring any musician from anywhere in the world to come and sing for them at the wedding.

"My wife said it had to be Luther Vandross. She wanted no one else but him. I tried several tricks to bring him back from the dead and, fortunately, one of them actually worked and he is here straight from heaven to sing for my beautiful wife," said the groom.

Then the lighting of the venue went off, leaving only the dim glow of the candles. Suddenly Luther appeared on stage, as tall and handsome as we knew him when he was alive. It was a DVD played through a data projector onto a white cloth that was hung across the stage. It was so real, as if he were indeed there. Tears fell from my eyes when his velvet voice sang "Always and Forever." It was indeed a fairy-tale wedding. The kind of wedding that made most single people wish they could get married.

Why had I never met a man like Mofeti? Why had I never had a wedding like this? I thought as I took the turn-off to Marishane. Driving into the church parking lot, I decided not to take part in the funeral proceedings as I had not known the deceased lady and wasn't that close to the priest's family. But mainly because I hated the endless speeches.

Everyone said the same things about the deceased. The situation was even worse if the person who'd died was an elderly person. The event swarmed with people who all wanted to give speeches. Individuals representing neighbors, the royal house, grandchildren, in-laws, church members, the burial society, and friends would narrate endless, pointless stories about the departed. In some cases, even a representative of the under-taker had to give a speech.

I decided to try to locate an old friend of mine, Ivy, who got married to a local guy some years back and relocated to this village. Marishane was really more like an urban township than a village. It was the only village I knew with tarred roads running through it. Unlike in most rural settlements, there were no shacks or lousy housing structures. Most of the houses were large and modern.

After driving around for a few minutes, a young boy at a four-way stop next to a dusty soccer field directed me to Ivy's place. I could not believe the house she lived in. It was a mansion with a yard that could have been two hectares wide, surrounded by high white walls. The house was painted lime green. On the one side, next to the pool, there was an entertain-ment area with a thatched roof and glass walls. Ivy said it was the part of the house that belonged to her husband. He had de-signed and furnished it himself. Inside there was a bar, lounge, study and bathroom. Animal sculptures and prints dominated the interior.

Ivy was very pleased to see me, even though this was just a brief visit.

"My old friend!" she cried.

At noon, while we were still enjoying our catch-up session, my mother sent me a "Please Call Me" message. I knew this meant that the funeral was over and it was time to collect her.

"You can't leave now, when I haven't seen you for so many years," said Ivy.

"But I will come and visit you properly and spend the whole weekend with you soon. This is the old lady's trip."

"I am going with you to fetch her. We are all going to have lunch here before you guys leave," she insisted.

"My friend, do you really want to spend your Saturday afternoon with an old lady? We won't be free to talk about whatever we want," I said.

"If that is what it costs to spend a little bit more time with you, that's fine. I don't mind your mom. In fact it would be nice to see her," said Ivy.

A while later we were all seated in the thatched lounge enjoying a mixed grill over another bottle of champagne. It was a pleasant reunion, and my mother seemed comfortable. Ivy, a teacher with a natural sense of humor, entertained us with stories from her school.

"Mama, you know learners these days are out of control. The other day our principal tried to discipline some latecomers and closed the gate on them. *Eish!* The naughty children pushed against the gate until it knocked him over. *Mxe!* It was most unfortunate, as he landed in the dust and he was wearing his favorite black suit which he told everyone was an expensive brand and was bought by his engineer son," said Ivy, giggling.

"I am glad I am retired now," said my mother. "That would have killed me. I always said that without the rod we can't get these children right. This thing of calling the parents to discipline children does not work in villages. The parents just don't come."

"*Hee!* My principal sometimes defies the law out of frustration and uses his *sjambok*," Ivy said.

"Really? But that is now a crime, *mos.*"

"*Theetsa!* He no longer uses it that often. Last week he chased two Grade Nine girls who were late with a *sjambok*. They ran and hid in the bushes outside their classroom. When he eventually found them, they were bending down from the waist, with their dresses over their heads. They had decided to scare him away by showing him their buttocks. When he came face to face with their smooth dark behinds, he ran away screaming. The unexpected sight overwhelmed him. He just could not use his *sjambok*. When he reached the staffroom, he was still in shock.

'*Sies!* These kids! They don't even wear panties. They wear *ntepa*,' he said with disgust. After the principal left the staffroom, one male teacher said, '*Eh!* The principal got to check out their G-strings.'"

Everyone laughed.

After some time, the conversation about lazy teachers and naughty secondary school learners turned to the topic of the funeral.

"Mama, did you know the old lady who died?" Ivy asked my mother.

"Yes, I did. I am very close to Reverend Mashatile's family," my mother said.

"I knew the old lady too," said Ivy. "I always saw her in church. *Ag* shame, she was a vibrant *magogo*. Always very active."

"*Yaa*, I was with her when we were called to a family meeting at the priest's home two weeks ago," said my mom.

"*Mma*, how come I did not know that you are related to the priest—you even attend their family meetings?" I joked.

"I was part of the delegation that negotiated and received *lobola* when his daughter Makau got married," she said.

"Oh yes, *mxe*, you told me! I had forgotten—I drove you to the wedding reception," I recalled. "It was the most romantic wedding I have ever attended. I remember I wasn't so keen to go with you, but I ended up enjoying myself."

"The *lobola* negotiation also went very smoothly. We asked for twenty thousand rand, but they paid double the amount."

"Wow! That is a lot of money. What does the husband do?" asked Ivy.

"He is an engineer and I understand he also owns a consulting business," said my mother.

"*Mhh!* Some people are lucky. And the girl?" I asked.

"She is a lawyer," said my mom.

"*Mhh*, nice," Ivy said.

"Not so nice. There is trouble in paradise. That is why the *lobola* delegation was called to another meeting."

"So soon? That wedding was last month, *mos*," I said. I wondered what could have gone wrong with that perfect couple. I remember feeling envious at their wedding. I'd also felt bitter because they'd made me feel like my life was lacking.

"I should not be talking about this. It's a family secret. But the truth is that the marriage was called off. Moruti asked us to take back the *lobola*," said my mother.

"What?" Ivy and I said simultaneously.

Handing back the *lobola* was a rare thing in our culture. In fact, neither of us knew anyone who had ever experienced it. In most cases *lobola* would be paid back to the husband's family only if the wife was at fault—for example, if she had been caught cheating or conceived a child that was not the husband's. Even in those cases, it was a rare occasion when the *lobola* was returned. Most of the time people just did not take it back. Usually the money had been spent and the family could not afford to pay it back.

The only instance I could think of where this had almost happened was with my friend Mmatau, in the early eighties. Her father bumped into her husband, who was enjoying a romantic meal with a girlfriend in a restaurant, having left Mmatau and the children at home. The old man got so angry that instead of confronting him, he took out his check book and wrote him a check for the amount he had paid for *lobola*. Mmatau's husband never cashed the check. Both her husband and father never mentioned what had happened. She heard about it for the first time more than ten years later.

Ivy and I were curious. We used all our charm to try to convince my mother to tell us more.

"No, I can't. It's a sensitive issue, a family matter, and I don't want to betray the faith they have in me," said my mother.

"But we are also family. It will be like sharing with your daughters, so that we never make the same mistake. We won't tell anyone. We just want to learn from what happened," I said.

"*Eh Mma*, it's true. We have to learn from the elders to become wiser about life's issues." Ivy winked at me.

We finally persuaded my mother to tell us. Apparently, the couple dated for less than a year before the wedding. Mofeti told Makau that he was sure she was the one and therefore he wanted to do things right. He said that because she was a priest's daughter, they should do things the Christian way and only sleep together once they were married and had been blessed by a priest in church.

Makau, who was twenty-nine, told my mother that she could not believe her luck. She had been dating men who played hide-and-seek when it came to commitment. Here was a man who was wealthy and who wanted to make her his wife. Yes, she would wait and do things the right way this time. It all made sense. He spoiled her rotten, treated her like a goddess. He was a breath of fresh air, after dating guys who were unreliable and with whom you had to climb over a roof and scream naked to get their attention and respect. With this guy, everything just flowed. She did not have the feeling she'd had in previous relationships, that she was trying to stop the rain or make a river run backwards.

All seemed well until the fifth week after the wedding. They were now living together in Mofeti's house in Polokwane. That Friday night, Makau told my mother, she did not sleep. She walked up and down their double-story house the whole night. All of a sudden, the fancy furniture did not seem as smart as she'd thought. Upstairs in their bedroom she watched Mofeti sleeping like a baby and felt something inside her that wanted to strangle him. All the love she'd ever felt had disappeared. She decided then that she could not stay with him under those conditions. The following morning, she packed her bags and went back to her father's house.

At six in the morning, Makau was hooting outside her parents' gate. The priest's house was in the same yard as the Lutheran church. No fence or wall divided the church from the house. In fact, the house was so close to the church that you could listen to a sermon while drinking tea in the kitchen.

The priest's neighbor, MmaMaja, told my mother that she came outside when she heard the commotion. Makau's father was opening the rusty gate, still in his pajamas and nightgown. MmaMaja said his white head with its uncombed afro looked like someone had poured mealie meal on it. He unlocked the big padlock while two malnourished dogs ran around the BMW, as if the car were an invader.

"*Sesi, goring?* Why wake us up so early?" he said.

Makau started to cry, like someone who had just been told that her husband died in a car crash. She drove into the yard and stopped in front of the gate. Her father opened the passenger door of the vehicle and joined her in the car.

Her head was on the steering wheel.

"*Sesi!* What is wrong? Where is *mokgonyana?*"

"I left him at home. Papa, *go padile.* This marriage can't work," she said. Minibus taxis and people were already passing by the gate, on their way to the taxi rank, which was not far from the churchyard.

"What do you mean? Come, let's go and talk in the church. Passersby will wonder what is going on." He led her from the car to the church. Inside they sat on the front bench, next to each other.

Later Makau told my mother about their conversation. She said she had never seen her father so shaken.

"I have a feeling that what you are going to tell me is bigger than me," he said, "but let us pray for God to give us strength to deal with it." His eyes had turned red and his face was pale like an unclaimed corpse at a government mortuary. He stood up and walked around, then stopped at the pulpit and began to pray.

"Lord, I invite you into my family. I urge you to protect this family, especially my little girl, and keep all evil spirits away from us. Be with this child of mine. Whatever problem she might be having, I leave it in your hands. In the name of Jesus Christ and the Holy Spirit, Amen."

He walked back to where his daughter was sitting. She was no longer crying aloud, but tears were running down her cheeks.

"Papa, I cannot go on with him. It's not working."

"What are you talking about?"

"My husband, Papa. I can't go on with him. I tried but I cannot," she said.

The priest turned towards her and looked straight into her eyes. "Don't worry, my girl. God is always on our side. Nothing beats the power of God. Whatever it is, it will be solved in the name of Jesus."

"Papa, it can't be solved. Even God can't fix this."

"Makau, have you killed someone? You are scaring me," said her father.

"Papa. That man. *Eish!* I don't know how to say this," she said.

"Tell me, my girl. You know you can tell me anything."

"Papa, *a go berekegi ka dikobong*. He can't perform in bed."

"What?"

She began to cry again.

"He is fine with all other things but the bedroom. Since the first time I met him, he has never done anything. Before the wedding, he said that he wanted to marry me first, but now it's been five weeks since the wedding and still, Papa, nothing is going on and he does not want to talk about it."

"What do you mean ... he does not do anything?"

"Papa, what do you want me to say? There is nothing going on."

"*Mh! Ke mathata!* This is a big-big problem, *sesi*. You can't live like that, my child. No, no, no, you are right. This won't work. There is no way you can live like that. Eh! Don't worry, I'll call the *lobola* delegation. I haven't touched his money. We can arrange for the *lobola* to be taken back. No young woman can live like that if she is married. If this man can't perform now, immediately after the wedding, he will never be able to perform. What will happen when you are forty or fifty? He is young now. *Mhh!* No! I see your point. This would mean that you, my girl, must run around searching for what he can't give you. Not with my daughter. We will give him his money back."

My mother told us about how the *lobola* delegation tried to convince the priest that maybe they should first try to seek medical help, like recommend a urologist or the Men's Clinic, but the priest kept on saying, "My daughter is not a toy. She is human. She deserves a real man, a real husband. I am not going to allow them to play my girl like a skipping rope. It will be a cold day in hell before I allow my daughter to be put through that. They knew he had a problem. That is why they doubled the *lobola*."

To the surprise of some, the delegation went ahead and took the *lobola* money back, and the marriage was dissolved.

"*Mma*, were you part of the group that took the money back?" I asked my mother.

"No! I excused myself, telling them that I was going to see my eye specialist in Pretoria. I could not do it. It was just too painful. But the priest told me they went ahead with it."

"I could never do something like that. If it was me, I would have just given some other reason, like he doesn't buy groceries or he doesn't pay bills. I would never humiliate someone like that. They embarrassed the whole family," I said.

"Things have changed," said Ivy. "I can't even imagine having that kind of conversation with my father. The words would never be able to come out of my mouth. And, Jesus, this man is a priest, but he did not want to even explore other options."

"I still think it's weird that we are discussing this thing with my mom," I said.

"That is why I did not want to tell you the story," said my mother.

We all kept quiet for a while, then she said, "You are human before you are a priest. Maybe he just wanted what was best for his daughter, like everyone else."

"And what's best is sex, Mma?" I said.

"If sex is good it makes up ten per cent of a relationship's health. But if it's bad or not happening, it makes up ninety per cent."

We all laughed.

"For a man like that one, I would have stayed. I am sure we would have eventually found a way to solve the problem. Whatever happened to soulmates and divine love? I mean those are the words they both used at their wedding," I said.

"So this girl was definitely not a virgin: she knew how sex is supposed to be. What was the problem, *gabotse botse*? Was it because it was too small or was it erectile dysfunction? Maybe there was absolutely nothing there?" said Ivy, and we laughed.

"Nobody knows. We were not told. That is not the kind of question you can ask," said my mother.

"You see, I believe in the old African traditional marriage where girls were married when they were still virgins. They did not know anything about sex and had nothing to compare their husband's performance to. Whatever the husband offered was perfect," I said and both my mother and Ivy laughed.

"You don't mean that," said Ivy.

I could not stop thinking that this man couldn't be the only one with that kind of problem. Now, if even priests did not offer support for such problems, where did this leave us? Were Christianity and God merely courteous formalities that people had learned to enjoy with mental and emotional detachment? Were those who were sexually challenged not worth being loved? I could not help imagining that the same problem must exist in many marriages, and yet people were living normal lives in spite of this. I was surprised by how people could be so unsympathetic. These people had sons. How could they be sure that they were not swimming in the same pond? I felt sorry for Mofeti, and tried to imagine how I would feel if I were him. It would have killed me.

The weekend ended and I went back to my normal life in Nelspruit. Two weeks later my mother phoned me to tell me that Mofeti had committed suicide before the divorce had been finalized. He hanged himself on his veranda and was found by the domestic worker.

I wondered how the priest must have felt.

Bridal Shower

Where I come from in Polokwane, Limpopo, bridal showers are called kitchen parties. It is an occasion where old and young women gather to socialize and celebrate the bride to be. They eat, talk, and open presents. There is no dress code. The conversations are led by the older married women, who are regarded as the most qualified to advise on what to expect from marriage and on how married women should carry themselves. You could be a psychologist specializing in relationship issues, but if you are not married, you do not qualify for this prestigious position.

"Marriage is not a mattress," "a man is the head of the family," "the best way to a man's heart is through his stomach," "a man is an axe—at times he must be lent out," and so on and so on. These were common phrases in those estrogen-fueled parties. Well, as a single person with no immediate prospect of marriage, I refrained from attending most of these apartheid-like events, where the non-married were not so subtly discriminated against. I always felt out of place, not to mention bored and irritated by the pitying looks from the married comrades and brides to be.

For this reason, I winced when I heard that my younger sister Katlego was to have a bridal shower. However, the invitation card, which was sent via email, made me suspect that this one might be different. Against a lavender background was a picture of a sexy woman wearing a G-string, a sparkly bra, and a circus hat, holding a whip in one hand. The dress code said "something purple and sexy." This was to be the first bridal shower in our family, and my other younger sister Bonang volunteered to host it at her home in Centurion, Gauteng.

Katlego was the lastborn child in our family, and her wedding was a very big deal. Already there had been a series of revelries and festivities. The *lobola* celebrations were as lavish as a wedding. There had been a big shindig at my home, with a marquee, speeches, and many cheer-leading relatives, friends, and uninvited guests.

I remember how proud my uncle looked when he gave his speech, dressed in his brand new light brown Carducci suit. He thanked the groom's family for marrying into our family. He then went on to embarrass all the females by telling the guests that the women in Katlego's family, on both the maternal and paternal sides, rarely got married.

Indeed it was true. My mom was the only one who got married. None of my aunts, from both sides of the family, were married. Bonang and I and all my female cousins were still single. I resented his referring to this fact because most of us were single by choice.

"The Mamashelas have blessed this family by marrying our beautiful doctor daughter, Katlego. We have given you pure gold," he said, addressing Katlego's in-laws.

Then there was another big-white-tent celebration at the groom's parents' home to welcome Katlego, the new *makoti*. Preceding that were two other small occasions where many Mokokoroshi chickens lost their lives. That was when the Mamashelas came to introduce themselves and negotiate the *lobola* price. Next was Thabang's bachelor party, followed by the bridal shower. And finally it was the wedding, a two-day celebration. But of all the celebrations, the bridal shower is the one that left a lasting impression.

I drove with my friend Judy to attend this occasion in Centurion. On the way there, we took pleasure in the different species of summer flowers that enlivened the margins of the N1 highway. Judy was one of those lucky women who married into money and did not have to work. She left her job as a systems analyst and became one of the most over-qualified housewives I knew, with a master's degree in Information Technology.

For Judy, the most strenuous decision of the day was which car to take her kids to school in, or whether to let the driver take them, or deciding on what the domestic worker should cook for dinner. The only setback in her life was a husband who was always away on business trips. When she complained, he told her that it was the price she had to pay for her luxurious lifestyle, which I doubt she would have traded for an ordinary life.

The normally three- to four-hour trip to Centurion from Polokwane took us two hours in Judy's car. She was wearing a pair of dark blue jeans with a lilac sleeveless top and I had on a lavender-colored dress. We thought we had done a good job of following the brief.

When we arrived at Bonang's place, most of the guests were already there. The cars parked outside took up most of the street. Strung across the gate was red tape, the type the police used when there had been an accident, and a sign that said "Danger: No Man Zone."

Bonang lived in the Thatchfield golf estate, where most of the upper middle-class of Centurion were entombed. Most of the houses were double-story and Tuscan in style. You seldom saw anyone on the streets except for domestic workers and gardeners. I wondered if these people ever went outside unless they were in their cars.

Judy strutted through the front door with her 50,000 rand Louis Vuitton bag swinging on her left shoulder. The guests were drinking, chatting, and laughing. Looking around, I realized that Judy and I had clearly overdressed.

The others were wearing very little: waist-length nighties and G-strings, lace-up corsets, teddies, and maids' uniforms with whips and handcuffs. I had never seen anything like it. I felt like a real *plaasjapie*, a case of Jane comes to Joburg. One girl with a large behind, who was wearing only a G-string, said, "Ladies, which part of sexy didn't you get?" They all laughed.

"*Ngwana mma*, you must slip into something naughty. That's the idea today. Get out of your Limpopo boxes and join in," said Bonang.

"I am not running around naked, even if you pay me. Forget it. I am not as young as you girls," I protested.

"I will wear a pair of Bermudas—that's as far as I will go," said Judy.

"Where's Katlego?" I asked.

"She is on her way here, she doesn't know anything about the party. Redi lured her away for the whole day—it's a surprise," Bonang told us in her bedroom.

We heard shouting from the living room.

"It must be her. Let's go."

The screaming crowd of about thirty women was already out at the gate. "Surprise, surprise!" everyone yelled.

I saw Katlego's big eyes protruding. "You *skelms!*" she said, hitting the friend closest to her and laughing. "You are all crooks. Why didn't you tell me?"

Her friends Tshepiso and Bonang pulled her into the bedroom, where a mauve *camiknicker* was laid out on the bed for her to wear.

"They have hired a stripper," Mmabatho, Bonang's friend, whispered into my ear.

"What?" I whispered back.

"You'll see. We are going to have fun. I can't wait for the stripper show to begin," said Mmabatho.

A stripper? She must be joking. There is no way. That is something you see on television, I thought.

Bonang and Katlego's friends had prepared a feast of African cuisine consisting of *mogodu tini*, oxtail, chicken and cow feet, mopane worms, *chakalak*a and pap.

"You better eat now, ladies, because once we get started there won't be time for food," said Bonang, wiggling her bare bum at the guests.

Bonang's dining room extended into the living area, where

the purple lounge suite and lavender curtains matched the women's outfits.

"Ladies! Shhh! Hey, can I borrow your ears? Listen, no cameras please. I will take some photos which you can get from me afterwards. But we are trying to avoid having half-naked pictures of us floating around the internet," said Bonang.

We then moved on to a hilarious game where people had to ask Katlego questions: What is your G spot? Tell us about your first time. Was he good? What is it like with Thabang? These were Mmabatho's questions. She shrieked and cackled with laughter whenever Katlego withheld a response.

"She must dance for us," said Mmabatho.

I was shocked at the questions, some of which I believed should not be asked. Little did I know that things were just warming up: worse shocks were in store.

I asked Katlego who her dream man was and she said Barack Obama. Almost everyone asked something except for Katlego's sister-in-law, Judy, and Redi. They just laughed.

For the next activity, the dining room table was decorated with matching fancy underwear. I assumed that these were presents until I discovered that the lingerie was for sale. A consultant, a glamorous-looking woman called Mary, gave us a short presentation on the prices and on how to wear the garments. "Girls, you have to buy Katlego some of these. She will need them to keep her man interested. And to keep him from the vultures that are out there," the consultant joked.

Next, she brought out a large bag from which she began to remove all sorts of gadgets. "These are a must-have for all women, especially Katlego." She took them out one by one and explained how each one worked, switching them on and off.

I had no idea what they were. I stood up from my chair at the back to get a better view.

"Times have changed. Today, as a married woman, one needs to play around in the bedroom, keep things interesting.

Gone are the days of the missionary position. If you don't make it interesting, you won't keep him at home," said Mary.

Among other gadgets, she showed us different types and sizes of dildos. There was the smaller one, which she called Billy, and the bigger one she called Vuyo. There were toys you could eat, such as edible underwear, oils, creams, handcuffs, whips and other strange objects I did not recognize.

She probed for questions and input. There were questions all right. "What if my man is always available? Do I still need Billy and Vuyo?" said Tshepo.

"Sweetness, he might always be there but there will be times when he might be tired or going through something. Then this toy becomes very handy. But you've got to know how to introduce it to him," said the consultant. "It is very important that it is the right size."

"What do you mean by the right size?" one of the girls asked.

"Did you see how big Vuyo is? Don't bring him if your man is smaller."

The girls fell on each other laughing.

The consultant added that there were other types of vibrators: like the egg-shaped ones that women keep inside them and that had a remote control to switch them on and off.

"Imagine getting a climax anywhere, anytime. *Mhh*! Imagine driving and you're stuck in traffic and you just press and enjoy life—nice and easy. You just keep it inside all day and press the remote whenever you feel like it."

Mmabatho giggled like a schoolgirl who'd just caught her first glimpse of a penis.

I stood there with my arms folded across my breasts. I said nothing but could not close my mouth. I had never been in a situation in which people were so open about such private things. I came from a different era and world where such things were taboo. I did not know quite how to feel.

"Is this this woman is not a prostitute?" I whispered to Judy.

I was taken aback when Bonang allowed two men in. They

passed through the crowded living area and were directed to the kitchen. The white one looked twenty-something and the colored man middle-aged. Neither seemed moved by the women's sexy attire. I figured that they must be the strippers Mmabatho had mentioned.

The consultant concluded her presentation and handed out business cards. "Anyone who is interested in ordering anything can talk to me later. I also give individual coaching sessions," she said. Most of the guests bought underwear as presents for the bride-to-be.

I saw the white guy disappear into one of the bedrooms. I went into the kitchen and poured myself a double whiskey. I had a feeling I was going to need it. Judy, who had been drinking fruit juice all along, decided it was time for a cider.

Tshepo, Katlego's friend, and the colored guy were busy on the laptop. I realized later that they were working on the music compilation for the night. It was the first time I'd seen music being played from a computer that was connected to home theatre speakers.

"You guys are late. You were supposed to be here at eight," said Tshepo.

"We had another show in Waterkloof and there was an accident on the N14 that blocked the traffic on the way here."

Everyone was now whispering about the strippers.

"Do you think they will get completely naked?" Judy asked, her eyes shining.

"No way! I don't think so. It would not be decent," I said.

"We'll see."

Tshepo pulled out one of the dining-room chairs and put it in front of the TV, instructing Katlego to sit on it.

She sat there in her *camiknickers*, facing the rest of us. We watched her like she was a TV show. She really looked sexy. This was not the shy, conservative Katlego that I knew. She was usually not much of a drinker, but I saw that she had a glass of vodka and cranberry juice in her hand. She kept changing positions to show off her new outfit.

"If your patients could see you like that, I am sure they would heal immediately," Judy said.

"You must mean the male ones. The female's conditions would get worse at the thought of their husbands being treated by you," Tshepo said.

"Fortunately I am getting married. My white-gold ring will cool them off." Katlego laughed.

The music started: the first song was "I like the way you move." I recognized it from the Vodacom ad, the one with that pot-bellied meerkat dancing like his life depended on it.

The white guy entered the living room, dancing as if he were on a stage in front of a thousand people. He was now dressed in green military shorts and a purple muscle top, through which his six-pack was clearly visible. It reminded me of a chocolate bar, two rows of neat compartments.

He appeared taller than when he'd arrived, and his brown hair was now tied back in a neat ponytail. He advanced into the crowd of women and began to dance in front of Katlego. His moves were like those of a guy trying to entice a girl he had met in a night club. He danced, swinging his waist to the left, to the right, and in circles, as if he had no muscles.

He looked at her with bedroom eyes, running his hands softly up and down her face. He moved closer, wiggling his hips up and down and sideways. His hands shifted to her shoulders, to her hips and legs. Then he did the unthinkable. He moved his lower body in circles, brushing against her bare stomach with his crotch. She closed her eyes and screamed. "*YOO NNA MMAWE!*"

The guy went on and on, ignoring her shocked reaction. The guests had moved from the sofas and dining-room table and were now circling around Katlego's chair. Everyone was screaming, "*Yoo! Yoo!*"

Tshepo jumped up and down with her hands stretched out, the way James Brown does in his shows. No one remained seated. Those who could not see jumped onto the sofas.

The stripper took out a chiffon scarf, which he used to caress Katlego's body, running it all over her.

She shrieked and closed her eyes, covering her face with her hands. The shouting grew louder. Listening to the screams, it was hard to tell whether the women were in danger or whether they were having fun.

The stripper moved on from Katlego and began to pick out some of the guests. He seemed to know who to choose, approaching Mmabatho first. They danced as if they had rehearsed together. Their lower bodies moved from left to right and up and down, lower and lower.

Then the stripper stopped dancing to remove his shorts, which he did with a single flourish, revealing a thong and a tight behind shaped like two big fists. It was fascinating to look at him from every angle. All the eyes in the room moved to the front of his thong, which appeared to be amply filled out. The girls' yells were now piercing. Judy and Redi were breathing heavily next to me, and I kept on saying, "*Ke mehlolo.* This is crazy." I had thought that I would have to die before I saw things like this.

He then pulled forward a young girl from the audience. She was wearing a transparent black nightdress trimmed with red fur and underneath it a matching G-string, also see-through. She was practically naked. She took off his top while they danced. I was now afraid of what might happen.

They danced almost lying down, on top of each other but without touching one another or the ground. They both balanced their bodies with one hand, their feet on the ground. They looked like two people in the act of sex. The yelling escalated. Everyone's eyes were glued to the dancers.

The sexy girl rejoined the audience and the stripper kept on dancing. He still had the chiffon scarf, which he moved all over his body. He then took off his thong, at which point all the women were jumping up and down and yelling at the top of their voices. We still could not see his thing, however, because he'd covered it with the scarf. He moved the scarf from side to side teasingly, allowing us glimpses of skin.

Everyone was now squirming with anticipation, and they moved closer and closer to him. He had hardly any space to dance as everyone surrounded him. Tshepo moved us backwards.

Mbabatho said, "Ladies, be patient. You will see what you want to see."

"I want to touch him," said Katlego's sister-in-law, who was leaping up and down next to me. She surprised me, because I knew her to be very quiet and reserved. She pushed her way through and touched one of the stripper's butt cheeks. She came back screaming, looking delighted.

The stripper removed the scarf for a second. There it was, and the screaming reached a shattering point. "We want to see it again," said Judy, and everyone joined in. "We want more! We want more!" The women chanted like they were on a service delivery protest march. The stripper kept on dancing. A minute later, he lifted the scarf again. And then the show was over. It had lasted thirty minutes, but it felt like only two.

Judy would not accept that it was all over. Redi said to Bonang: "My cousin, I know you are full of surprises and tricks. But today you have outdone yourself." Questions began to flow to the organizers.

"Where did you find him? How much did he cost?"

The colored guy, who was still leaning on the kitchen counter, was happy to answer all the questions. He gave out business cards.

"We also do individual shows that are R300 for ten minutes. If you like, we can do one now, for anyone who's interested," he said.

The show that we had just seen had cost R2000 for thirty minutes. Bonang then said, "No private shows in my house. Those who are into private shows can do so in their own homes."

"Ladies, are we really letting him go? How about another

show?" said Judy, putting R500 on the table. "Pitch in, ladies, come on. Thirty more minutes."

Another R2000 was collected and the show went on. The girls were even crazier than before.

At the end of it, I found Judy and Redi asking the colored guy if it was possible to call him to come and perform in Limpopo. Later I saw Judy and the stripper chatting, both of them scrolling through their cellphones.

"Ladies, where there's money, we go. We can even perform in Ghana for you, as long as you have the bucks."

Although my whole being was shocked, I realized and accepted that times had changed and that I came from a different age. I thought about the kitchen parties I was used to but could not imagine this crowd listening to some old lady telling them clichés like "a man is an axe—at times he must be lent out." I tried to picture them unwrapping gifts, glass, and tea sets that they did not need.

No, I could not see it.

On our way back to Limpopo, Judy spent most of the trip giggling into her phone.

"You want to come to Limpopo next week?" she said with a chuckle. She then told the person on the other side of the line that this was not a good idea. "I will invite you when there is a bridal shower." She laughed again. "You want to visit me personally. Hahaha!" The conversation went on until we approached the Manthole Traffic Control area and she saw traffic cops.

Six months later I received another sexy invitation card for a bridal shower. This time it was yellow and the dress code was stated as "strictly lingerie," venue: Polokwane, Tender Park. Judy was going to host a bridal shower for her younger sister Mokete, whose wedding was in December. It would be the first of its type in this conservative community.

My Perfect Husband

A man cheating on his wife in our community did not make headlines. Infidelity was as commonplace as taking a bath in the morning. In most cases, the girlfriend automatically assumed the status of deputy wife. The community accepted her as the official *nyatsi* even though the man did not marry her. She could even conceive two or more children with the man and he might provide a house for them. Then she would be accepted by the man's family, especially the parents and siblings. Any woman who left her husband because of a *nyatsi* was considered an idiot.

"Where does she think she can get a man who does not cheat? All men cheat, it's in their nature." This was always said in our township.

The more affluent a man was, the more women he would have. The chances of finding a man who did not have a *nyatsi* were as slim as winning the Lotto. Men now felt even more justified because President Zuma had four wives and possibly a higher number of *nyatsis*. It was simply accepted as African culture. Some women had tried to take it up with their mothers-in-law and all they got was: "He is better, he has only one *nyatsi*. His father had five *nyatsis*. And look! I am still here. You just have to live with it. Be grateful that he is still supporting the family."

Nevertheless, you would still get a few men that were honest and true to their wives. When a man was like that, though, it was assumed that he was just better at keeping his affairs secret. "There is no way he cannot have a girlfriend. He just knows how to hide things," they would say. A wife to such a man was considered fortunate and privileged for not knowing.

Most women knew their husbands' *nyatsis*. Some women fought tooth-and-nail with them, but those who did not were considered to be well-mannered and mature. Most women lived with the pain of sharing their men and family resources with these *nyatsis*.

I was one of the few lucky women in Sibasa township. My husband Mashudu was a decent man. There were no official or unofficial *nyatsis*. He was a devoted father and husband. He had never been unfaithful.

Mashudu was a tall man, with a slim figure, who preferred to dress in formal attire at all times. Be it Monday at work or Saturday while reading the newspaper on the veranda, he always looked immaculate. He was a man with personal dignity, humility, and common sense, and also a man of monkish self-discipline. My bond with my husband was as sturdy as two intertwined trees with joined roots. Mashudu was respected by everyone in our community. Most women regarded him as the model husband. If they could, they would have traded in their adulterous spouses for him.

"You are the luckiest woman in the world. If all these men were like Mashudu, this world would be a better place," my female colleagues often commented when they saw him dropping me off at work.

Mashudu was the kind of man that came home every day straight after work. He was also a sober-minded man who took neither alcohol nor cigarettes. If he was not at home, I always knew exactly where he was. We went everywhere together: the shops, church, funerals, and weddings. People called us the finger and nail couple. Up to now I couldn't even drive because he took me everywhere I wanted to go.

I was a teacher at Sibasa Primary School and Mashudu was the education circuit office manager at the Sibasa circuit office. He was a church elder at the Mbilwi Lutheran church and was also the chairman of the building committee. In our house, we all went to church every Sunday. After the sermon, my husband walked to the pulpit holding the black announcements book close to his chest. My husband loved things to be written and documented. He would lay the book open on the pulpit and button up his jacket. It was as though he would not be able to read if it remained unfastened. After clearing his voice, he would begin to read, embellishing the announcements so that each one took as long to read as three. People would listen attentively because his voice commanded your attention. Then when he was done he would start a chorus in his capable tenor, urging the congregation with his hands to join him while he danced his way back to his seat. After church he greeted everyone, offering the aged and disabled a lift home. His disarming smile displayed his perfect white teeth.

About a year ago, one showery Friday morning on our way to work, he told me he had been invited by the department to go to Pretoria that Sunday to attend an Outcomes-based Education workshop. The workshop was to commence on Monday morning and would continue until late on Friday. He told me that he planned to visit his uncle in Mapetla township, Soweto, on the following Saturday and would be home a week later.

My husband was the kind of man who hated food cooked by people he did not know. It was difficult to get him to even enter a restaurant when we went shopping in Makhado. He said he doubted the hygiene of such places.

Mashudu loved simple traditional food. I decided to prepare provisions for him to take on his trip. I bought two live Mokokoroshi chickens and slaughtered them. I then removed their feathers and cleaned their insides. Sunday morning, I woke up at four to boil them because they always took forever to cook. He was to leave at eight in the morning. When the chickens were ready I fried them in their own fat so that they would stay fresh for days. I also prepared *mutuku* porridge, which was his favorite and was known to last for three to four days without a fridge. A whole cake tin of *mutuku* and two full chickens and a bowl of *moroho* would last him, I thought. I knew he would probably not like the food they cooked for them at the hotel.

On Sunday morning, I served him his favorite breakfast of *mutuku* and fried chicken insides. Mashudu was a porridge man who never ate rice or bread. He licked his fingers after eating his meal with his bare hands. He then washed his hands in the blue enamel basin which I placed on his much-loved chair.

"No one can cook *mala* like you do, my dear wife. That was a wonderful meal," said Mashudu, drying his hands with the clean yellow kitchen cloth.

My two sons carried his bags and the provisions out to our car. As he drove away, I watched him through our mesh wire fence with a feeling of misgiving that I could not explain.

"Don't forget to find out if they can keep the food in the fridge for you." These were my last words as he left.

Monday afternoon I went to the choir practice at our church as usual. My heart almost skipped a beat when I saw Mashudu's twin brother Ntakuseni. His tall figure with its large stomach blocked the door. All of a sudden I could not sing. It felt like there was something stuck in my throat. For a while I continued to hum the song. Then I recalled that Mashudu had not phoned the previous night to tell me that he had arrived safely. I was not worried about him because he was the kind of man that didn't care for cellphones. Most of the time, he forgot his in the car.

I stepped away from the inquisitive eyes of the choir and hurried to where Ntakuseni was standing. He looked gloomy. He took my hand and directed me to the car. I left without saying goodbye to the choir members.

"Ah, *khotsimuhulu*," I greeted him, "why are you here? Is there a problem?" I said, expecting the worst.

"We shall talk at home. Mashudu is waiting for you there. My mother and father are also there," he said.

"What is wrong? Is everything OK? Is Mashudu OK?" I asked.

"Mashudu is fine, but there is a problem. Don't worry, it's a solvable one. But only you can solve it. We will talk at home," said Ntakuseng.

The five minutes' drive felt like forever. I knew my brother-in-law well enough not to probe any further. I knew he was not going to tell me what was going on upfront. When we finally arrived at home, he almost bumped into a neighbor's son who was playing soccer with my two sons in the yard.

We walked straight to the main bedroom. I could still hear the boys' voices when we reached the door. Inside I found my mother- and father-in-law together with Mashudu. They were sitting on the kitchen chairs and Mashudu was on the bed. His eyes were red and his expression grim. He was still wearing yesterday's clothes. His black trousers and white shirt looked soiled. When I came in, his eyes fell to the carpet. I could feel heavy words and thoughts in the air even before anyone said anything.

I knelt down on my knees, clasped my hands together, and bowed my head to greet my in-laws appropriately.

"Aah!" I said, still kneeling.

"Aah!" said my mother-in-law.

"*Ndaah!*" said my father-in-law.

"*Khotsi a* Tshiandze, why are you back so soon?" I said. I then raised my head but remained seated on the carpet. I had to look down because as a daughter-in-law it would have been rude to look my in-laws straight in the eyes.

"Tell her what happened," said my father-in-law to Mashudu.

"My dear wife," he said, his voice trembling.

"What is wrong?" I asked. He looked down again and breathed heavily in and out.

"This is the most difficult thing I have ever had to tell you, but there is no other way," Mashudu said. "There has been a terrible accident. Our car is a write-off."

For a while I kept quiet. *That is why his clothes are in such a state*, I thought. The air was still heavy.

"Well, we must thank God. A car is nothing. We will get another one," I said.

He was quiet.

"There is more. Tell her," said my mother-in-law.

"Someone else was in the car," said Mashudu. "She did not survive."

"She?" I asked.

"Yes. Mark Mulaudzi's wife, Matodzi," said my father-in-law.

"The accident happened last night, just before the Kranskop Tollgate. We were hit by a truck whose brakes had failed," said Mashudu.

"I see," I said.

There was silence again. I was confused. I wanted to ask questions. Matodzi Mulaudzi was a nurse. Where could she have been going? Was he giving her a lift somewhere? My in-laws and my husband avoided my eyes. I kept quiet and waited, hoping to get some answers.

"The major dilemma is that Mark and his family up to now have not been informed. Mashudu is the only person who has this information, other than the Bela-Bela police. Mashadu promised the police that he would inform the family in person, as we are all family friends. So he cannot go there alone to report this. It won't look good," said my father-in-law.

"I see," I said.

"It will look bad if they are told that it was just the two of them in the car. Mark might be suspicious or angry. You know how people are. They could interpret it negatively and Mashudu might be in trouble or, worse, they may even kill or bewitch him. My dear sister, you know how the Venda people are," said Ntakuseni.

I felt hot and cold at the same time, like someone who was having hot flashes. It was then that I understood what was going on.

"So we will all accompany him to the Mulaudzi home. The story is that you were with them in the car. It's the only way we can get out of this whole thing," said my father-in-law, as if we had all been part of what had happened.

The disturbing and sad part was that they were not even negotiating with me. I was simply given instructions on what I had to do.

"I need time to think about this," I said.

"There is no time to think. A person is in the mortuary and her family has not been informed. We must go now, before this whole thing turns into a mess," said Ntakuseni.

"OK, I need a minute with my husband," I said. "Mashudu, can we talk in the other bedroom?" I got up and he followed me into the children's room. I closed the door.

"There is no other way. We have to go together," said Mashudu.

"I need the truth before I get myself involved in your muddle. Was she your ..."

Before I could finish asking the question, Mashudu said, "Yes, she was. It was a big mistake. I am sorry."

As I was trying to process what he had said, the family came into the room without knocking.

"Let's try and solve this issue, *mazwale*. The other things we will fix later. You need to protect your family, for your children's sake," said my father-in-law.

I went along with their plan. It did not feel as if I had a choice. I watched my husband lie to Mark. I watched Mark crying like a little baby for his wife. It was sad. After a while Mashudu's story began to sound convincing, even to me. That was how effective his lies were. He said that we met her at the taxi rank where she was to board her taxi to Johannesburg, and offered her a lift.

While we were there, I learned that Matodzi had been off duty that whole week. She had decided to go and moonlight at Morningside Mediclinic in Johannesburg to make extra money.

Matodzi was buried the following Saturday, survived by her husband and five children. The lastborn were two-year-old twins. On the surface, I appeared calm. I did not want to look as much of a fool as I felt inside. I was so bitter about the whole thing that when I looked at Matodzi's twins in the church's front row, I thought they looked like Mashudu.

Ntakuseni's wife, who was seated next to me, did not make it any easier. She kept on pointing at the two small girls. "You see those two girls in the front row wearing the identical velvet dresses? Look at them carefully—can you see them? They are Matodzi's lastborn twins. Look there next to the lady with a green hat," she went on.

My husband had attended workshops once a month. I discovered that Matodzi had always worked the night shift, which gave her two free weeks a month. She used one week every month to work at Morningside. Ntakuseng's wife was the one who gave me all this information. She seemed to find it all very amusing. Ntakuseng had an official *nyatsi* whom she knew very well. She also knew the *nyatsi's* twin boys. She was glad to welcome me into the league of cheated-on wives.

After we had informed the family about the death, my husband refused to talk about the issue. Pursuing the topic was as pointless as using sign language in the dark. He continued with life as if nothing had happened. We went back to our perfect married life and he continued to drop me off at work every morning and accompany me to church every Sunday.

The only thing that changed was my friendship with Mark. We kept in touch.

♥

The Threat

"Please God, let it be a ghost," I prayed when I opened my eyes and saw a slim figure standing next to my bedroom door. It was five in the morning on Friday, 5 May, on a farm located halfway between Nelspruit and White River in Mpumalanga.

"She is here," the young man spoke softly, giving the impression that there were others present.

At that moment, I was not afraid. I jumped out of bed and shouted "Hey!" at the top of my voice, thinking I would scare him away.

Then another slim figure appeared. It was then that it became clear what was happening. These were not ghosts. I wished they were.

They were young, maybe in their early twenties, skinny and covered in dirt, as if they had been walking on a dusty road. One of them was wearing a cap that obscured his face and the other had bloodshot eyes.

"What do you want?" I asked, boldly approaching them. They pushed me aggressively, practically throwing me on the bed, pressing my face into the mattress. I fought to move my head to the side.

One of them took out a gun and the other one was carrying a knife from my kitchen. When I saw the gun, my courage faltered and I realized that I could get killed. From that point on, I became a cooperative victim, following all their instructions.

Could it be that they want to rape me? I wondered. I decided that if that was their intention, then I would let them do it—without fighting back—to avoid a violent rape. "Are you guys going to rape me?" I asked in the politest voice I could muster.

"We're not here to play games. We are here on a job," the guy with the gun said in Seswati. Being a Sepedi-speaking person, I hadn't realized until that morning that I could under-stand the language so well.

"Guys, I see no point in attacking me." I tried to stay calm. "You can see there is no one else here and the alarm is not working. There is no danger for you. Just take whatever you want and leave," I said.

"We want money. Where is the money?" said the guy with the bloodshot eyes, rubbing the gun against my face.

I picked up my handbag, which was lying next to my bed, and took out all the money I had (about R300). Then I led them to the other bedroom and took out another R200 from the closet.

"This is all the money I have," I said.

I kept on engaging them in conversation as they moved through my house, taking one belonging after another. The guy with the knife was carrying items in one hand and holding my arm with the other. They took whatever they thought was valuable and piled everything onto the kitchen table. "Hey guys, I know life is tough. There are no jobs. That is why you're on this job," I said, engaging them in small talk. They just stared at me, looking amazed. I kept on chatting and asking questions. "Where do you come from? You guys seem like nice people," I said as we were rushing in and out of the kitchen.

After a while I asked the guy who was holding my arm if he could let me go for a while because I needed to smoke. The guy with the gun was furious when he found me alone in the kitchen, smoking.

"Are you crazy? How you can leave her alone? She will press panic buttons and we will get into shit," he said.

When we were in the living room, the guy holding my arm examined my hi-fi speakers.

"Are they working?" he asked, pointing at them. When I confirmed that they were, he said, "Mm, they will look nice in my room." He then disconnected them and added them to the rest of the stuff in the kitchen.

I was still not that scared; it felt like I was acting in a movie. All that seemed real were the eyes of the guy with the gun. Something in them told me that if I made one mistake, he would kill me. They collected whatever they perceived as valuable but also left items that were worth taking. The microwave, laptop, digital camera and leather jackets—all that stuff was right in front of their eyes. That made me realize that they were also panicking. They only had an hour before daybreak.

The worst part for me was when I realized that they were planning to transport the stuff with my car. When it was time for them to leave, they could not find the house and car keys. As they were carrying things, the guy with the gun had placed the keys and my cellphone in the side pocket of his trousers and had forgotten about them. He kept on emptying his front and back pockets. I helped them to look for the keys, although I knew exactly where they were. I was thankful that they weren't able to take my van.

I suggested that they leave through the kitchen door, which led to a garden flat attached to the house. That way they would use the flat door to exit. I gave them the spare keys to my Alfa Romeo, knowing the car had a tracking device. They were running out of time and the smaller car meant they could not carry everything.

Up till then we had been getting along fine—before the guy with the gun decided they had to tie me up.

They were taken aback when I refused.

"There is no way you are going to leave me tied up on a farm. I'd rather you shot me with that gun."

I suggested that they should lock me up in one of the bedrooms, untied, and leave with the key.

"Look, this woman didn't give us any problems," said the guy who had held my arm. "Let's lock her up untied."

"Be careful with my car, it has a tracker. If you keep it for too long they will find you," I said to them as they rushed out. I thought that might scare them and compel them to abandon the car sooner.

Five minutes later, at seven minutes past six, I was out of the house, after managing to break the door down, and had called the police from my neighbor's place.

I thought my encounter with the criminals was over. Little did I know that this was just the beginning. Nevertheless, I considered myself lucky because of the attention I received from the men of the law. In South Africa, most people who experience crime whine that the police don't really help them. Enough has been said about the police being inadequate. But I experienced the opposite with the White River police.

Fifteen minutes after my cry for help, three police vehicles arrived in my yard: the inspectors, a dog unit, and the fingerprint guy. Thirty minutes later, about eight cars were crammed in my yard. Black and white police officers roamed all over the place, most of them in uniform but some in plain clothes. I appreciated their presence, which distracted me from the trauma of the incident. They were all shocked by my calmness. They kept asking each other, as if I were not there, "Is she the lady that was robbed?" They were everywhere. They had taken over my house and my yard, asking all kinds of questions.

After writing down a statement, the tall, pitch-black man who appeared to be in charge of the fingerprint team asked me to show him where he might find the burglars' fingerprints. His eyes, mouth, nose and ears were all larger than average. His voice was authoritative and instructive. "Lady, if you can't remember what they touched, you make my job difficult," he said.

At that time, my thoughts were just floating around. I remember imagining what he might look like when he was angry, how animated those big features would become. I was convinced that if someone owed me money and I took him along to collect, the sight of him would inspire them to pay without any excuses.

He eventually found some fingerprints on the fridge. The guy with the gun had pushed against it on his way out. Suddenly the officer's face lit up.

"This is a good one." His smile didn't look like a grin, more like someone battling to swallow steel wool. "We got him," he said, dusting black powder onto the fridge. He kept on talking to me as he proceeded with his job.

"What language do you speak?" he asked in the same way a traffic cop would ask for your driver's license.

"Sepedi," I replied.

This answer seemed to change his attitude towards me. "I am from Bushbuckridge." He smiled, less of a grimace this time. "I can speak Sepedi. Why do we torture ourselves trying to speak the Queen's language? You know, I'm sure they thought it was a white person staying here, otherwise they wouldn't have dispatched so many cars." He chuckled at this. "I am surprised they didn't send a helicopter." He turned away from the fridge to make sure no one else was listening. "You must be the only black person living in this forest. What made you choose to stay in such an isolated area?" he asked.

I wasn't sure if he was laughing at me or at whoever dispatches cars from the White River police station. I was now feeling irritated and chose not to respond, but he continued laughing and joking about the issue. A colleague of his took pictures of the fingerprints and him standing next to them. Then I had to sign some papers that had the fingerprints pasted on them. The last police car left at about noon.

From that day, the White River police patrolled the main road at night and at times they would go to the extent of driving up to the farm to check that all was well. Inspector Grobbler, who was the investigating officer, popped in every now and then to update me on the development of the case.

I thought I was OK and was very grateful that the criminals had not raped or harmed me. But Saturday and Sunday passed and I could not sleep at night. Whenever I closed my eyes, the burglars reappeared in my dreams, knocking at my bedroom window, telling me that they were back. On Monday morning, I was the first patient to arrive at my GP's surgery.

"I am not prescribing sleeping pills for you. You need a psychologist," said the doctor.

"But I'm fine. I'm just tired. Please, I don't need a psychologist, I'm not crazy. I've just been robbed," I said. "Going to see a psychologist won't work for me. It is so self-indulgent. It's for bored rich people. I'll be fine, doc."

Dr. Otto Mcacwa, who is also a good friend of mine, was not impressed by what I said. He insisted on giving me a sick note for the day, which I had to submit at work. He phoned a psychologist and booked an appointment for the following day. He also arranged that I get my medical certificate from the psychologist.

I was surprised at the outcome of the first session. The man knew exactly how I felt, what I was still going to feel, and why. That was something I hadn't expected, educated as I was.

"For starters, on a practical note, you need to intensify the security systems in and around your house," said the psychologist. "You're not going to be able to sleep when you feel unsafe."

Three days after the robbery, the criminals were arrested. They were traced through their fingerprints. The guy with the gun was actually a dangerous criminal wanted for murder. Most of my belongings were recovered, including my car and hi-fi speakers.

I was tired of all the bureaucracy and wanted my life to go back to normal. I now knew all the procedures that one went through after being robbed. It was the fifth day after the burglary and I had spent the day with another branch of police that dealt with retrieving stolen cars. Identifying my car was a tiresome ordeal, with all kinds of documentation needed. After all this, I had to go back to the police station to fill in another form in Grobbler's office. It had been a long day. I was irritable and tired when I walked into the inspector's office, which he shared with his colleague Joubert.

Grobbler's desk faced the door while Joubert's formed an L

shape, extending to the window. When I walked in, Joubert was standing next to Grobbler's desk and they appeared to be discussing a document. When they saw me, they reacted the way I would have if I'd seen a ghost. I was too exhausted to analyze their response or let it bother me.

"How are you, madam?" they said simultaneously and looked at each other. Then their eyes moved away to a space in the corner of the room before swiveling back to me.

"I need the forms. I want to get this over with," I said.

Grobbler handed them to me quietly. They continued to look at me strangely. I perused the form while moving to sit on the chair closest to the door. It was then that I noticed the other person in the room. I could not believe it. There he was—the guy who had held the gun to my head five days ago! His torso was bent so that his head was almost level with the floor.

"It's him, the robber!" I said.

The inspectors nodded without saying a word.

He was handcuffed. I pushed aside the middle chair that separated me from him and stood in front of him.

He kept looking down. I was suddenly no longer tired.

"Hey, why aren't you looking at me? Look at me!" I said, and he lifted his head, stared at me briefly, then lowered it again.

"You thought you were clever the other day and now you can't even look at me. Heh? Heh?" I raised my voice. The two officers stood next to the desk, frozen. I felt the urge to inflict some kind of pain. I looked around for an object to throw at him and was tempted to push Joubert's desk, with all its files and papers, on top of him. I came to my senses and remembered that I was in a police station.

"What did I do to you? Who sent you to my house? Do you know me?" I bombarded him with questions. I was shouting so loudly that officers from nearby offices came out to see what was happening.

"You have blundered, boy," I said. "I am not a white man. I am going to deal with you the African way," I shouted. "I went to Zimbabwe to consult my *inyanga*. He told me that you won't live for long, you and everyone you sold my stuff to. You messed with the wrong person this time. They should just release you to enjoy your last days," I said on my way out, pushing my way through the crowd standing at the door. "I will bring the form tomorrow, inspector. I have had enough shit for one day," I shouted.

I hadn't thought I was capable of acting like this. I knew that the threat of witchcraft would disturb the thief, because most black people in Mpumalanga believed in such things. Considering what I had gone through, I thought my behavior was justified, and yet it did not make me feel better.

A week later I came face to face with the other culprit in an identity parade. I thought it was going to be like in the movies, where there was glass between you and the suspects and they could not see you. I had to identify him out of ten pairs of criminals' eyes piercing through me as if I was the bad guy. They looked at me with eyes that said, "If I get out of here, I'm coming for you." That was scary, and for months I was traumatized, seeing those faces in people I met on the streets.

Three years passed before the case was heard in court. The criminals were denied bail because of their other cases.

My threat fell on fertile ground. I never believed in witch-craft and certainly hadn't consulted any traditional healer. It was just a lousy threat, but evidently it worked. The guy who bought my TV from them died mysteriously—a headache, and he was gone. Then one of the culprits got sick in prison and died.

Grobbler and Joubert made a special trip to my house to inform me about the deaths, and wanted to know specifically what I had done. They were fascinated by the whole fiasco. The court staff summoned me during recess and the interpreter asked me which *inyanga* I had consulted.

"*Eish, sesi,* your *inyanga* must be very powerful," he said, gazing at me with admiration. "Where do you come from?"

I just walked away smiling. I never bothered to explain

myself, because I knew they would not believe me.

When I eventually faced the remaining culprit in court, he had already spent three years in prison. I felt that was enough punishment for the crime, but it was not up to me.

My anger had diminished and I pitied him. The case was remanded three times and when eventually it was held, he still could not look at me. He'd had a disagreement with his lawyer, who was provided by Legal Aid, and had decided to defend himself. I don't know much about the law, but I gather that he did not do well. I did not attend the sentencing, but when I left the court, it was clear that he would get a minimum of fifteen years in jail.

I wondered what had led him to this kind of life. Something must have gone terribly wrong in his upbringing. It was sad: no family member or friend attended the court proceedings.

But watching him in the dock that last time, it was remorse more than pity that I felt. He looked thinner, weak, and defeated, much like his friend and colleague had looked weeks before he died.

A Million Dollars in Grahamstown

A wise man said that the human species can survive without anything, apart from human affection. Something I took for granted, as all my life I'd existed in a crowded environment, where human affection was readily available. It was only when I decided, at the ripe age of forty, to go and study at an institution 1500 kilometers away from home that I realized what I'd had.

I spent the first four months alone, with only a few arctic relations with the erudite to sustain me. It was like living in a graveyard. I then met someone and agreed to go on a date on a Saturday afternoon. I was thirty minutes late. He waited for me at Raglan Road next to the Chinese shop. It was a cool autumn day and I was dressed in a caramel cashmere coat with grey fur.

I wasn't sure if I was really interested in this date. But I was feeling exasperated with academic life and I needed a distraction. I wasn't looking to get involved. I was just there to check him out, get to know him.

The man I was meeting was extremely handsome. He was not an academic, so I regarded him as a breath of fresh air. At forty-six, he was six years older than me and implausibly single. He was tall with a good physique and was always well dressed. His bronze skin was flawlessly smooth, as if it were licked by some magical creature every day. He had a long face with chiseled features.

I had met him at the municipality when I was doing research for an assignment. He seemed to know everyone there. They all knew his name. Although I wasn't sure exactly what he did, he projected himself as someone important. He always referred to his busy schedule. There was a vagueness in all he said, as if he had a need to impress. *But maybe that was just me being my cynical, analytic self,* I thought.

When I was in my apartment preparing myself for the date, I thought about a conversation I'd had the night before with Tebello and Jenny. I was attending a class party hosted by our American lecturer Denise. Other than the lecturer, the three of us looked to be the only golden oldies over forty at the party.

We secured a corner in the kitchen. Talk of our children soon moved on to men. It did not take us long to realize that we were all single and looking for someone. Tebello revealed that she'd almost found Mr. Right that week.

"Where?" we all asked at once.

"Here in Grahamstown," she said.

"Really?" said Jenny

"*Eish!* It's a long story," said Tebello.

She told us that a friend of hers, a psychologist at the local psychiatric hospital, came to her apartment to inform her that she had found Tebello the perfect man. The friend said that the guy was single and in his fifties and was from her workplace. Tebello told us that she was very excited and assumed that it was a colleague—probably a doctor or a psychologist.

"I thought that God had finally found my address. My prayers were being answered. I wanted to meet him straight away. Can you guess what happened?" said Tebello, choking with laughter.

"OK! You met him. You liked him. He liked you too and you all lived happily ever after," I said.

"Well, to make a long story short—the man was a mental case at the hospital. Apparently, he lost his mind after the sudden death of his wife. He never recovered. My friend wanted me to go out with a mad man!" Tebello said. We all laughed, even though I did not think it was funny.

"But maybe if he has a new wife, he will be fine," I said.

"OK. No problem. I will tell my friend to arrange a meeting for you. You can be the new miracle cure wife," Tebello said.

"Looking for a man at our age, here in Grahamstown, is like trying to find a million dollars," said Jenny wistfully.

"Speak for yourself. I think there are good men that we can go out with here," I said.

"You definitely haven't lived here long enough to know what I mean," Jenny said.

As I drove to where my date was waiting for me, I thought about Jenny's words. "A million dollars." I had not told her that I may have just found my million dollars in Grahamstown. I had to be sure first if it was for real. I wondered what could have happened to Jenny for her to come to such a hopeless conclusion. It was clear that she had given up on any prospect of ever finding a man in Grahamstown. I eventually decided that it must be a white thing that did not apply to us blacks. It couldn't be her personality, because she was a lovely, sweet lady. As I was pondering this, my cellphone rang. It was him, my million-dollar man. Something in me wished he had grown impatient of waiting and left.

I recall then that he had not mentioned where he was taking me. I was annoyed with myself for not having asked. His friend's white van was parked like an abandoned car outside the Chinese shop. It was dark by then and Raglan Road looked deserted. There were no pedestrians passing, as there were during the day. I parked behind them.

"Let's follow him," he said as he climbed into the passenger seat of my car. I drove behind the friend's car with no idea where we were heading. We stopped at his friend's house. I remained open-minded about his undisclosed plan for the night. Every now and then our eyes met accidentally and we both smiled, but his smile was somewhat remote. I began to feel uneasy.

"I am glad you came. I was not sure you were going to make it," he said, searching for the button to adjust the seat as his long legs were uncomfortably touching the dashboard. After spending half an hour waiting outside his friend's home, we left.

He directed me towards the township. I was surprised, as

I had imagined he lived in town. The young and old, the drunk and sober, donkeys, cats and dogs, speeding minibus taxis, and donkey carts competed for space on the narrow road. I opened the window and could feel the dust. He directed me to a house in the Joza section. I still did not ask about the plan for the night. I decided that this was an opportunity to get to know him better by letting him be himself. We ended up at a dilapidated old house.

Inside, there were three rooms including the kitchen, and there was another bedroom outside. There were several people in the small home. He simply introduced me as his friend Mapula. I was welcomed as if these people had known me for years. I found this vaguely unsettling, as I had never heard anything about them. Two men who later turned out to be my date's friends were drinking peppermint liqueur.

I was then bombarded with all kind of questions. Where do you come from? Where do you work? Where do you stay? And so on.

"She is from Rhodes," my date said. This statement seemed to cover all their questions.

"*Mhh!*" said a middle-aged woman, who was sitting on an armchair. Everyone turned to look at me. Even the girl who was sitting behind the sofa came out. Theirs were eyes of admiration. I felt like I was Paris Hilton—famous for nothing. We hung around there for half an hour.

When my date eventually excused us and told them that we were going somewhere, they all walked us out. I have never had people that impressed by me. I realized that they were even more impressed with my vehicle than with me. They gathered around my ordinary Opel Corsa, gawking, as if it were a Rolls Royce or a Porsche.

Thereafter we went to meet a friend of his at a tavern. He mentioned that this friend was politically connected.

"We have to go there because this friend of mine is going to buy us drinks," he said.

♥

The friend did not come and he suggested that we should go to my place.

"I will buy meat and drinks. We can go and cook it at your place. I will call my friend to come and collect me later," he said.

His presence warmed my small bachelor apartment at the postgraduate village. He spiced and grilled the meat while I cooked the pap. We ate, listened to music, danced, and ended up spending the night together. After the long drought of human affection, I felt like the sun was sleeping in my apartment.

I was pleased, even though his lovemaking was self-fulfilling. Everything revolved around him. He never tried hard to please more than himself, and I don't think he even pleased himself completely. I did not know what to make of it. I consoled myself by thinking that he would learn gradually, with time.

I could not help thinking about something Tebello once said about handsome men not making good sexual partners. She alleged that they were narcissists who only cared about themselves. She believed that the uglier ones tried a lot harder. Tebello also maintained that a man's behavior in bed was a reflection of his personality and what he would become in a relationship. If he was selfish, it was most unlikely that he would be generous and considerate in the relationship. I thought this was all pop psychology founded on unproven notions. This relationship was going to work. I felt like I could do to him what spring does to flowers, what summer does to fruit trees.

By now I had given him a nickname which he seemed to like. I called him MD, short for million dollars. He never asked me what it meant or why I called him that. He probably thought it was short for managing director. He always told me that when the mining projects that he was facilitating kicked off, he was going to be the MD.

The morning after, when he woke up, he found me already working on my laptop. He asked me if it was OK for him to take a shower. He stayed in the bathroom for two hours. Passing the door, which he'd left open, I saw him dancing like a five-year-old in the shower.

"This was the nicest shower I have had in a long time. You know we don't have water in the township," he called to me, rubbing his body with Radox shower gel.

"Where did you buy this? It smells so nice," he said.

"Clicks," I said. "It has a feminine smell. You will smell like a woman the whole day."

I saw vulnerability in his eyes. They were the eyes of a small boy. He continued dancing around the shower. I wondered how a man who flew to all locations in the country with the mayor could be this fascinated by a lousy shower.

After bathing, he washed the previous night's dishes. This was new to me. I was used to dating wealthy men who wouldn't wash a dish even if their lives depended on it. Maybe this was not so bad—after all, I was forty. Maybe this was the time to try something different.

Later, when we were having our breakfast, which he made, I asked him questions about the liberation movement Azapo, which he said he'd served all his life. He did not tell me much. Several times, he mentioned that he had been a political prisoner in Johannesburg. He seemed to enjoy talking about the mining project more.

I learned that he had never married. He had four children with four different women, two of whom were conceived at the same time. I was not surprised, as it was the norm for most black men his age to boast about the number of kids they had. They flaunted their children (even when they did not support them) the way other people boasted about their university qualifications.

He told me that he lived in his late parents' home (the house in Joza) with his sick brother and his fifteen-year-old son. He never asked me anything about myself—not even what I was doing at the university.

For most of the conversation I listened, interjecting only

when I could not understand his Xhosa-flavored English.

"You know, I am serious," he told me. "I have been looking for someone I can settle with. I don't know you that well, but I see potential in you. If we are to be together, will you be able to adapt to the Xhosa culture?"

I wondered how easy that would be. I looked into his eyes for some sign that would show me he was being sincere, but he was hard to read.

"I don't know," I said.

After he left, I reflected on my philosophy on love. *Maybe this was the time to redefine it*, I thought. Maybe it was time for change—time to revisit my standards and criteria for evaluating suitable men. Maybe I had missed out on a lot by being too fussy and analytical. Perhaps for once I needed to sit back and let things happen, be spontaneous. If I got into any trouble, I could see it as an adventure.

In our subsequent meetings it was clear, without anything having been said, that we were in a relationship. Although I was extremely busy at the university, I made time to see him every day for an hour or two. Within a week, he had introduced me to all his relatives and friends. The first two weeks were almost perfect. We met for meals at his place or in town. We laughed, talked, and kissed, the way new lovers do. But still something in me would not allow myself to let go completely. I didn't introduce him to anyone, not even Tebello. I wanted to wait—to be sure.

I was impressed but also taken aback by the fact that his house, small and bare as it was, was so clean. The plain floors were always shiny and the surfaces spotless. You could hardly believe that only males lived there. My place was never that neat. Most of the time, I had to jump over papers and clothes to find my way around. Sometimes he would clean my apartment, saying that he understood that studying while working part-time could be strenuous and didn't leave much time to tidy.

It was on the third week that our cozy love affair began to show cracks. On the Wednesday, at about ten in the morning, my cellphone rang. I was in the library and had forgotten to put it on silent. I jumped and immediately switched it off, embarrassed.

It was him, Mr. MD. I went outside and called him with my last ninety cents airtime. He phoned me back.

"Hello! *Ukuphi?*" he said.

Whenever he called me on my cellphone, our conversations were hurried and straight to the point. It irritated me. I thought it was unromantic, but I never complained. *Maybe he is saving his airtime,* I thought.

"I am in the library," I answered.

"Are you not having classes today?"

"At eleven," I said, adopting his business-like tone.

"Until when?"

"Five."

"OK. Give me your car. I need to go somewhere urgently," he said, as if he were asking to borrow a nail clipper.

"What?" I said, as though I had not heard him right.

He repeated his words.

"I am afraid I won't be able to do that," I said.

"Why?" he asked, raising his voice.

"My sweetness, I would never lend anyone my car, not even my mother," I said.

"Why? Please, it is a serious issue. It's about the mining project," he said.

"Listen, can't I drive you there during lunch or after five?" I said. He then put the phone down.

Well, maybe his airtime is finished, I thought. I developed an instant headache.

After classes, I phoned him but he did not answer.

I called him the following day and he sounded fine. That week we only spoke on the phone—no meals or kisses. I had seen him every day since our first date and now it felt like I was being punished for not giving him the car. I'd seen what happened with friends who'd lent out their cars, and I had told myself I would never get into a situation like that. Either the guy would have an accident while drunk, and then discover he didn't even have a license, or he'd disappear with the car, returning only when he felt like it. Or worse, he would use the car to impress other women or even to commit crimes.

I did not see MD until late on Friday afternoon, when he asked me to come and pick him up. He spent the weekend at my place. I tried again to explain to him why I couldn't give him my car. I even made up a story that the car belonged to an ex-boyfriend who had given it to me on condition that it would not be driven by anyone else. He gave me a cool look and smiled the distant smile he'd worn when we first met. A few minutes later, he said, "Don't worry because I am going to buy a car soon. I have saved about 50,000 rand towards that. So you can relax. I don't need your car. It's just that it was an emergency. But normally I don't have a problem with transport. I have access to my brother's car. He lets me use it any time, but he was away recently."

That night when we went to sleep, there was no action in the bed. Normally I slept in his arms but this time he turned to face the wall. Still, our bodies could not help touching as my bed was small. In the morning, he woke up and took his usual long shower. I made him breakfast and dropped him at the Monument, where he said he was attending a seminar. I then went into town to do my Saturday shopping. An hour later he called.

"Hello, *ukuphi?*" he said.

"I am still in town," I said.

"Good. Listen, at lunch I am coming with my cousin, who is also attending the meeting. He wants to meet you."

I was always humbled and seduced by how he liked showing me off. With my exes, it took years before any introductions were made.

"Ok, that's fine. Must I prepare something to eat?" I asked him.

"No, they have catering here. Bye."

Two minutes later, the cellphone rang again.

"*Mamela!* My dear, buy us some Jameson whisky. I will give you the money at lunch. We just want to get a shot before going for the afternoon session," he said and dropped the call. I did not know how to react to the request.

I didn't know him that well. What if he did not give me the money? I decided to give him the benefit of the doubt and went to the bottle store. When I discovered that Jameson whisky cost R290, I changed my mind. *This man does not even have a toilet inside his house, but he drinks alcohol this expensive?* I thought. I drank cheap dry red wine that cost R25.

When they came to my apartment after lunch, his cousin did not even get out of the car. He came in alone, hoping to collect the whisky. When I told him that I had not bought it, he said nothing and just left, slamming the door on his way out. That day MD did not come back as he'd said he would, or even phone to say he was no longer coming. I took it as a blessing in disguise, because I had an assignment to finish. I realized that he was gradually becoming an assignment too.

Monday, Tuesday passed and he did not call. I also kept my silence. I was too overwhelmed by schoolwork to worry much about him. On Wednesday around lunchtime, he called. We met in town. I waited for him in the car next to the CNA bookstore.

"Do you have classes this afternoon?" he asked.

"No, the prof's not around today. He's postponed his class till Friday," I said.

"I need a favor. Can you take me to my son's school?" he said.

The school was in Juranti township, a ten-minute drive away. MD told me that they were suspending the boy until he came to the school to discuss his son's performance with the teachers. It was May, and they had been calling him since the beginning of the year. He had always sent his younger sister, who'd also dropped out of the same school. He wanted me to come in with him, but I preferred to wait in the car.

Apparently, his son had not been doing any classwork or homework. He defied his teachers and went to school only when he felt like it.

MD was very upset when he came out. We stayed parked outside the schoolyard for some time as he told me what had transpired.

"They were shocked that it was my child. You know they respect me a lot. The problem is that I travel frequently with the mining project. One week I am in Joburg or Cape Town or Durban. I am always away," he said. I had been with him for about four weeks and I had never heard him saying he was going anywhere.

"Where is the boy's mother?" I asked.

"She is married and staying in Cape Town," he said.

I went home with him and offered to help with the child— I was a teacher by profession. I checked the boy's workbooks and most of them contained only one or two exercises that had been completed three months ago. I agreed with the boy on a schedule, which I would monitor daily. MD just sat on the sofa watching soccer while we worked at the dining-room table.

The following Friday, Grahamstown's blue sky dispensed its tears all day. It was not raining cats and dogs but lions and leopards. At about ten in the morning, the "*ukuphi* call" came. He wanted to know if I had classes.

"Yes, I am going to be busy until five in the afternoon," I said.

"I need a favor, there is something extremely urgent. Can you give me your car?" he said.

This disturbed me a lot. *Is this man an idiot?* I asked myself.

"What?" I said in a loud voice, hoping it would embarrass or discourage him. No. He repeated what he'd said as if it were the most normal thing.

"Look, I thought we had settled this. I can't give you the car. This car belongs to my ex-boyfriend and I promised that I would never let anyone drive it," I said.

"But he is not here. He won't know," he said.

"It's not about him knowing, it's just not appropriate. I will never do it."

This time I dropped the call first. Why was I lying? Why did

I feel guilty when it was my car? Why did he feel entitled to it? What was I dealing with here? Did he have no pride—that trait so characteristic of men?

That Friday he did not call or visit. This time I was worried, and that evening I phoned him. He was drunk and playing very loud music. I missed him. *What exactly am I missing?* I thought. I could not answer the question. I focused on my assignments. It was the last week of the term and there was a lot to finalize.

On Saturday morning, I received another call asking for a favor. I was beginning to cringe every time he called. In fact, they were not even calls anymore; they were "Please Call Me" text messages. Then I would phone him, only to be asked a favor. One night he texted at midnight asking me to collect him from a friend's place in town, where he had been drinking. I stupidly woke up and went to collect him. The following day there was another "Please Call Me," and when I phoned he said, "Give me your email address. Someone is going to send me information about the mining project."

"No! I can't do that. I would rather help you set up your own," I said.

"Give me" had become his favorite words. He used them so casually, as if he did not know another way of asking. That bothered me. And the words "thank you" did not exist in his vocabulary. I was not sure if I might have encouraged this behavior in some way. At times, I would cook or buy food and eat with him, his brother, and his son. I am from Limpopo and we have a proverb that says that "food is the dirt of the mouth." It means that when you give people food, you don't lose anything. Could this have given him the idea that he was entitled to everything I had?

I later concluded that his way of speaking might be a Grahamstown thing, because even beggars here always said "Give me two rand" in an arrogant tone. Unlike the Limpopo and Gauteng beggars, who asked humbly, "Good morning, madam. May I please have two rand? I need to buy bread. I am hungry."

Although his favors and demands were not substantial (by

my standards), they were endless. It was as if he sensed that I was not going to hang around forever and therefore he must get as much as he could from me before I disappeared. I was not as worried about his string-pulling as I was about the fact that it did not embarrass him to ask for so much.

One day I was in the chemist when he texted and I responded as usual. This time he said he had forgotten to buy airtime for his son. He wanted me to buy it and text him the pin number. I was scheduled to meet the boy that afternoon. I bought the airtime. Five minutes later, the phone rang again.

"Can you phone me back now? I don't have airtime," he said.

I called again. My being in the pharmacy inspired him to be creative.

"I am not feeling well today. I have stomach cramps and my sugar is high. I also have a terrible headache," he said.

"Did you see a doctor?" I said.

"No."

"How do you know it's those things—maybe it's just *babelas*," I said.

"Well, I don't know," he said, ending our conversation.

Three minutes later, a text message came through with a list of medication that he wanted me to buy for him. I laughed to myself and ignored it. It was clear that we came from different worlds. In my family, on both the maternal and paternal sides, there was not a single man that depended on a woman. They preferred to be providers. Even when they were down and out, they would find it difficult to allow a woman to assist them.

That afternoon when I dropped his son at home, I found MD watching soccer with two of his friends. These friends were always at his house. They were drinking, talking, and laughing loudly. The one friend irritated me to the core. He had a sinister grin and a patronizing look.

Unlike MD, who was always neat and stylishly dressed, this man wore the same ragged clothes every day. He seemed to be proud of his poverty status. He was the kind of person whose look made you feel like you were being a fool. He laughed in a crude way, even when nothing was funny. Foam escaped the sides of his lips every time he opened his mouth. I tried my best to understand their friendship. Although I didn't express what I really thought, it must have been obvious. The two friends never tried to engage me beyond falsely cheerful greetings. I got the feeling that whenever I was there, they went out of their way to be even louder.

I needed to check MD's son Musa's books to see if he had done the work we'd agreed on. While I waited for him, I sat at the dining-room table. MD stood up and came over to me. He had a furniture shop catalogue in his hand. "We need a microwave, a proper stove, a toaster, and an electric kettle," he said. "I want you to help me choose."

"Electric appliances are overpriced in those shops. You can get them for 40% less at Game stores," I said.

He smiled and said there were no Game stores in Grahamstown. I did not want to know why I was being told about appliances.

Fortunately, the boy came in then and MD went back to his bickering friends and the soccer game. But ten minutes later he was at the table again, interrupting our discussion.

He hugged me from behind the chair and smiled. I had grown afraid of his smile. He was the kind of person who seldom smiled. He was so handsome that he did not need to.

"You guys are working hard, I must reward you," he said, and was seconded by his foam-mouthed friend. "Yes! I am buying supper. My dear, what do you want to eat?" he said.

"Anything is fine."

"OK, right, give me your car keys. I'll go buy at Pick'n'Pay. I will be back just now," he said, loud enough for everyone in the room to hear. His two friends and his son raised their heads to see how I was going to react.

"He is not going to Port Elizabeth. He is just buying from Pick'n'Pay," said one of them.

Something in the way the men looked at me made me feel trapped. I gave MD the keys and out he went. I regretted the decision the minute I handed them to him. I could not concentrate on his son's homework anymore. I was angry with myself more than with him. I could not understand why I'd given him the keys.

I sat there with my face in my hands. The thirty minutes he took felt like two days. He came back with a plastic container of food in one hand and two six-packs of beers in the other hand. I was so angry. I did not even eat the food.

"Thanks for the beer, my friend. My throat was beginning to dry up," said the foam-mouthed friend.

I decided it was time to leave. That night he abandoned his friends and came with me. He was in a good mood. I was still angry. When we got to the apartment, I went straight to my laptop. I switched on the TV for him and worked on my assignments until five in the morning. He kept waking up every hour or two asking if I was not coming to bed. I just looked at him and told him that I had to work.

I was woken by him at noon talking on his cellphone. He was directing someone to my place. He asked the person to call him from the main gate.

He turned to me and said, "I am meeting someone for a few minutes. It's about the mining project."

I nodded without saying a word.

"Give me the car keys," he said.

"What did you say?" I said, pushing the covers aside and getting out of the bed.

He was sitting on the cane chair in the corner of the room, putting his socks on. "I am just going to the gate. I'll be back now-now," he said.

"No! The gate is a two-minute walk. You don't need to drive," I said.

"I can't walk in this complex without you. I don't stay here, remember. The security officers will think I am a burglar," he said.

"Oh, but you can drive in here without me? No!" I said.

His eyes scanned the room, as if he was looking for the keys. I could now see anger building up in his eyes.

"*Unjani wena?*" he said. "Why are you threatening this relationship?" His words sounded strange, as if he were talking about a protest march. I was now sure that my neighbors and the security guards could hear him. He looked at me and repeated the question. "If you think you are frustrating me, this is nothing. I have been tried and tested by many women before you," he said, collecting his few items. He then banged my door on his way out.

I was too exhausted to care. He knew I had promised to come and assist his son that afternoon. I phoned the boy around midday and told him to expect me around seven in the evening. He told me that his father had been drinking since he came home and had hit him.

That evening when I arrived, I found MD with his friends drinking beers and watching soccer. The house smelt of home-cooked chicken. I went in and greeted them. They responded with their usual fake friendliness. I sat down and explained that I had an appointment with the boy.

"He is not well today. I have just given him headache pills. He must be sleeping," said MD.

A girl emerged from the kitchen. She could have been in her early twenties. She did not greet me or even look at me. She wore a pair of tight jeans and a short tank top that revealed a flat stomach and perfect young breasts.

"I need to schedule another appointment with him," I said.

MD stood up and went outside to the boy's room. I followed him as he went through the kitchen and the girl walked behind us, but stayed in the kitchen, where she was making something on the two-plate stove. When I turned to look at her, I could see she was sizing me up.

"For how long has he been sleeping?" I asked. When the boy heard my voice, he unlocked his bedroom door and came out.

MD went back into the house, leaving the kitchen door open. While we were still chatting, the girl peered around the kitchen door and then banged it shut. I almost cried when Musa came out with his face swollen and his eyes red. He told me that his father hit him because he was out when he came home.

He confessed to me that he wanted to live with his mother but the problem was that his mother's husband did not want him. I told him that he would have to arrange with his dad to allow him to come to campus for the homework sessions, as I wouldn't be coming to his home again. He cried like someone who had lost his mother.

I went back to the living room and bid my farewells. The girl was chatting and laughing with the foamed-mouthed friend. As I left she stood up and went into the kitchen again, her perfectly rounded buttocks rolling rhythmically as she walked.

MD followed me to the car. He stood a meter away from my window and smiled. It was a different smile from the "I need a favor" one. This was his inscrutable smile, the one that disappeared from his face like a light being switched off. His stare was blank, almost hostile. I opened the car window and asked, "Is that girl your girlfriend?"

"Why are you asking me such a question?" he said.

"Thank you," I said and then switched on my car radio and drove away gracefully. I tried to hold back the anger I felt but I was burning inside. Mostly I was furious with myself.

I remembered Tebello's words: "A shack will always be a shack—even if you try to put paint on it or dress it up with fancy furniture and curtains. Whatever angle you look at it from, it will never be a mansion." Even after realizing that I was pursuing a shack, I had kept on looking at it as if it were a mansion. I could never say I was seduced or mislead—this person had consistently shown me who he was. I just refused to believe him. After meeting the girl, I now understood why the house had always been so clean.

My heart ached. My mind told me I should be relieved, but a part of me could not help feeling guilty. Maybe I'd tried to force him to be who I wanted, someone he was not. I closed my laptop as I could not concentrate. I went to see Tebello.

"Some of these men are just not worth the trouble," she said.

"What do you mean? Everyone deserves to be loved," I said.

"That man is messed up. He doesn't deserve you, and he knows it. When a person realizes they don't deserve you and you fall for them anyway, they lose respect for you. They think you are a fool. They know that if they were you, they would never settle for someone like themselves," Tebello theorized.

"He had a rough childhood. His father died when he was eight. Maybe no one taught him how to be a man," I said.

"Hey, my friend! You are not a psychologist. So in a relationship, you must be a girlfriend not a therapist. You are not qualified to fix people. That fool was going to mess you up, bury you alive. I know his type. This is how it starts when people end up being abused by men."

I had to find a way to make peace with it. I needed to look at it from a different angle. I told myself he was what I'd needed at the time.

A few days later I was contacted by his son's mother, urging me to continue helping the boy. She even offered to pay for my services. She told me her story with MD. It was worse than I thought.

"The truth is that he is not capable of staying with only one woman. That is the reason I left. It was that and his violent nature. You were lucky he did not lay a hand on you, but I am sure it would have eventually got there."

Weeks later my million-dollar man came to see me, dangling a "you are the best thing that has ever happened to me" carrot. I did not buy it. He went on and on about how sorry he was and that the girl was not his girlfriend. He said he'd thought that if he could make me jealous, I would love him more.

Still today, he sometimes gets drunk and calls me. With

time, my anger and guilt has subsided and I have accepted him as part of my history. When we meet in town, I smile kindly. I've learned that as much as we cannot survive without human affection, we also can't survive on love alone.

Boy Toy

My first meeting with Vusi was strange. I was woken one morning by a knock on my door. It was early, and no one knew my new address, I thought. Maybe it was my new neighbor. I pulled the curtain aside and saw a male figure standing by the front door. *Mhh*? Not too shabby. I grabbed my red morning gown and rushed to the door.

A tall, fine-looking Xhosa man was standing there when I opened. "Hi, *uphilile*?" he greeted. "Sorry for waking you up. I am your new *makhelwani*. That is my cottage." He pointed to the front door of the small rectangular white structure next to my home. The garden flat faced south, making an L with mine. "Where do you work?" he asked.

I was taken aback because I thought people first established your identity before occupation. *So it was true what Ntombi had said about today's men*, I thought. "They want to know where you work before they take an interest in your name. If you don't work or have a lousy job, then there is no need to know your name," she'd said.

I invited him in but he refused, telling me that he was on his way to work. We stood at the door talking for about twenty minutes. I discovered that he was working for the engineering department of Makana Municipality. He did not reveal any specifics, but he had studied at the Walter Sisulu University of Technology in East London. He was originally from a village next to Mthatha.

"Are you married?" was his next question.

This was a question I always reflected upon before answering.

The reason it was asked would determine the answer I would give. Saying yes would protect me from all kinds of vultures—those who viewed being single as a weakness and an opportunity for exploitation. He did not strike me as that type of scavenger.

"No, I am not married. I am in a relationship with a very good man at home in Limpopo," I said.

"I am still single and looking. Don't you have friends that you can hook me up with?" he said.

"You must be joking. My friends are way older than you. A nice young guy like you should be able to do better than that," I said.

"No! In fact, I prefer older women. The young ones are trouble. You must introduce me to your friends. Tell them I am looking for a steady girlfriend," he said, smiling. He had small slanted eyes that almost completely closed when he smiled.

"Mmhh! I am not really the match-making type."

"OK, we will talk next time. I'd really like to meet your friends," he insisted.

I watched him through the glass pane as he made his way to his car.

I remember thinking that this was too much for me to chew before breakfast. All of a sudden, I could not go back to sleep. I found myself thinking about Robert Frost's line, "good fences make good neighbors." I sensed that I might need to keep properly maintained fences between me and this good-looking young neighbor of mine.

One thing I have always being lucky with is having good neighbors. Although I believe in "good fences" between neighbors, I have always struggled to maintain them. The friendlier the fellow citizen, the weaker the fence would be. When people told horror stories about their neighbors, I would be shocked because I had never been that unlucky. Although this might be a bit of a digression, I can't resist mentioning what happened with my friend Themba and his neighbor.

A new black woman had moved in next door, and Themba and his wife were excited. For years they had been the only darkies in West-End suburb in Nelspruit. Themba and his wife went round to welcome the neighbors the following day, bearing a cake tin full of freshly baked muffins. After all the usual introductions, the new neighbors revealed that they had moved from the nearby Thulani township, which was about thirty kilometers from Nelspruit. Themba told the lady, who was a single mother and an empowered woman working in government, that they were happy to have her as a neighbor.

"At least now there is someone we can have afternoon tea with, not like with these white people who are uptight and keep to themselves," said Themba.

The lady interrupted him, pointing out that this was the main reason they had left the township. She told them that the privacy and uptightness of the white people was exactly what they needed. Themba and his wife excused themselves, and after that initial meeting, they never spoke to the couple again. A few weeks later, the neighbors erected a tall wall that made it impossible for them to see each other.

After the day Vusi introduced himself, I avoided him. My gut told me that he was trouble. In Sepedi, they say that to avoid smoke inhalation you have to stay away from it. I could not curb my curiosity about him, though. I soon discovered that Vusi was a busy man. Almost every day he had different female guests. A fancy car in the parking lot and soft female voices would announce the visits. The journalist and writer in me could not ignore these activities.

Women of all shapes and forms visited my neighbor daily. They were thin, fat, old, young, ugly, beautiful, tall, and short. They all seemed to be wealthy. These women came at different times. Some spent the night. The ones that fascinated me the most were those that came during the day, particularly at lunchtime. I would see them tiptoeing in like teenagers in their high heels and power suits.

Two weeks passed without our paths crossing. At times Vusi would stand outside my door and shout, "Hi madam! How are you?" and I would respond without opening the door or even peeping through the window. Then I would hear his footsteps moving towards his cottage.

One Friday night, Vusi came round and found me enjoying my meal with a glass of red wine, sitting on the front doorstep. It was not yet dark. In the Eastern Cape, the sun set just before eight in the evening during the month of February.

"Hey! Long time. You always hide yourself in that cottage. It's nice to finally see you," he said, smiling and looking at me with a naughty twinkle in his eye.

I felt uneasy. I was wearing a very short skirt which I would never have chosen to wear in public, especially not in front of him. I continued eating my meal, eyes fixed on the food.

"I am not hiding myself. I am just working. I have a lot on my plate," I said defensively.

"Whatever," he said, walking towards his cottage

He came out, this time wearing only his underwear. He held a bucket in one hand and a few pegs in the other. He walked past me, smiling, to the washing line. His upper body was like a rugby player's and his behind fit and masculine. He was wearing a pair of tight white jockstraps. *If this whole pageant was staged to seduce me, it was a non-starter*, I thought. For me, a girl from the bush province of Limpopo, walking around half naked was inexcusably inappropriate.

"Mmhh! The air is nice here. These cottages are very hot inside," he said after he had finished hanging up his clothes. He pulled over the garden bench from the lawn and placed it next me.

I looked at him with questioning eyes.

"You look surprised, what's wrong?" he said.

"Surprised? Oh no! I am not surprised. Why would I be surprised?" I said, sarcastically.

He grinned.

♥

"Don't you think I am too old to be charmed by your nakedness?" I said casually.

He laughed again. "You know, when I am at home I don't like wearing clothes. Even this underwear is just too much for me," he said, standing up from the bench.

"Please don't take that off. I have seen enough of you. Just go...go get some clothes," I said, distressed.

"What do you take me for? I could never seduce you. I am a decent person," he said. "When am I going to meet your friends from the university?"

"My friends are white," I said.

"I have never tasted a white one. Seriously, you need to introduce me," he said with enthusiasm.

"Well, I would never fix you up, not even with my enemies," I said to him.

He laughed. "Why?"

"You seem to have enough women. In three weeks, I have seen more than ten different women park their extravagant cars in our driveway, and most of them only leave the next day. Why would I introduce my friends to someone with so many women?" I said, looking straight into his eyes. He laughed. I had expected him to be embarrassed.

"So you are watching me like a hawk," he said.

"No! Why would I do that? I can't help seeing them driving in and out."

"So you have seen the cars. My women drive powerful cars. I like powerful women," he said, animated.

"So why do you need my friends if you have powerful women?" I said.

"But nothing is serious with them. I want someone I can have a serious relationship with," he said.

"What makes you think my friends fit that category when you have never met them? And anyway, what type of woman qualifies as serious to you, if I may ask?"

He was quiet for a few seconds. "That is a difficult one.

Well, she must be powerful, good looking, and not too showy," he said.

"I see."

"Did you see the charcoal Alfa Romeo on Tuesday? It's a more recent model than yours. It's a nice car, hey? She lives in PE. Damn, she is a full house—a real full package."

"What is a full house?" I asked.

"She is coming tomorrow, I will introduce her to you. You'll see what I mean. She is a powerful machine that comes with all the extras," he said.

While I was still trying to absorb what he was saying, he changed the subject. "Tell me about you. You said you have an embassy in Limpopo."

"An embassy?"

"*Yaa!* A serious boyfriend."

"Well, my life is not as colorful as yours. He is neither a full package nor a full house. No gripping stuff. Tell me more about your PE full house with extras."

"You know this town is boring. You must set up another embassy here. Just for entertainment, otherwise you will be bored to death. I can introduce you to some nice guys," he said.

"Boredom is my thing. It's actually a good thing for me. It gives me time for my studies. Relationships are like a master's degree: a lot of work. I am not clever enough to handle two degrees at the same time."

"It does not have to be a relationship. Just a roll-on. Something to balance you."

"Some of us can't have flings. We get attached. I don't do flings and never will."

"Never say never."

"I am 42-years-old and I know exactly what I mean by never. Anyway, I have to go back to my studies. Thank you, this was a refreshing conversation."

"No, man! It's Friday, you must take a break."

"Good night," I said, going inside and closing the door.

"OK," he said, still sitting on the bench.

The following day, I bumped into Vusi and one of his "power houses" at Pick'n'Pay. They were buying cooked food. I was dishing out some tired-looking leafy vegetables from the salad bar when I heard his voice.

"Hello, neighbor," he greeted me.

"Hi, guys," I said with an exaggerated smile. He introduced her. It was the PE "full package," I realized, noting the Alfa Romeo key dangling from Vusi's hand. She had a full-figured body. She was neither beautiful nor ugly, just an ordinary middle-aged woman who could have been twenty years older than him.

The following week, my car refused to start—something to do with the computer box. This resulted in me walking the four kilometers to and from campus while my car was at the mechanics. When Vusi heard this, he offered to give me a lift until I got my car back. Traveling together helped me to get to know him better. Our conversations mostly revolved around him and his many women. I was amused by how he seemed to feel they increased his status.

One Tuesday he brought a very loud one home. That day there was no car, which was unusual. I normally didn't hear much from his house, even when he had women over, but that night I could hear everything this woman was saying.

The next morning, he was quiet. I decided to ask him about his flavor of the day. "My friend, yesterday you brought a different type to your normal taste. This one is not a full package... no fancy car," I said.

He looked at me, almost choking with laughter. "*Eish!* A typical Xhosa woman...very loud."

"If I could understand Xhosa, I would be telling you what you guys were talking about. I could hear every word loud and clear," I said.

"She is from the township. She is not my type. I don't like loud women. She talks too much. At tea-time, I am taking her back. She will never see me again," he said.

"Are you dumping her just for talking too much? *Ag* shame," I said.

"*Eish!* Another thing is that I have to go and fetch her from the township and take her back. It's a lot of work. I don't have that time."

That afternoon when we returned, Vusi was restless again. He kept trying to call someone on his cellphone but was not getting a response.

"*Nxa!* You know this girl is playing with me," he said, looking quite disturbed. "She is not answering my phone calls."

"Which one?" I asked.

"The East London one, the Volvo one," he said. "Let me try her with your phone. I have to talk to her. I am worried. The whole week she has not been answering. I don't understand what's going on," he said.

I gave him the phone, but there was still no response.

"Where is she working? Maybe she is under a lot of job pressure," I said, trying to cheer him up.

"No, but she always gets back to me," he said, hitting the dashboard with his fist.

I continued probing to try to get more information about the Volvo woman. I discovered that he had spent a weekend with her at the Fish River Sun two weeks back and ever since, she had not been taking or returning his calls. He told me that he and Miss Volvo had had a thing going on for two years now. He said he liked her because she was not as demanding of his attention as the others. They only met once in a while. She was also very generous.

She paid for all their escapades and always bailed him out when he had financial challenges. She was a municipal manager in East London.

"She helps me with serious things like rent and my car installments. She is my Minister of Finance," he said. "You know what! I love powerful women. I like it when we are in a bar and I don't have money, and she takes over, takes out her gold card and pays for everything." He spoke with the passion that I have seen other people show when they talk about their jobs. I listened without saying a word.

"Most Xhosa men are afraid of powerful women, but I am not. In fact, they fascinate me. They turn me on. I am good at getting them hooked on me," he said and then paused for a moment. His voice became deeper. "I have dated different types of successful women: doctors, members of parliament, businesswomen, both single and married," he said with his lower lip extended in a boastful way.

"How do you charm them?" I asked him.

"I just have a way with women. They love me. I have what they need and they have what I need. Introduce me to any successful women, the most disciplined or a devoted wife, I tell you, anyone, and I will bring her down. She will sleep with me."

I sat there wondering how someone could be so sure of himself.

"I now want a big political figure, a minister or a premier. I know I will get one. It's just a matter of time. This time you won't just see fancy cars in our driveway, you'll also see security officers," he said, laughing.

Without thinking, I found myself asking him, "Why?"

"For fun. Just to prove to myself that I can. Ya! Maybe they can create opportunities for me. You know, like connect me to tenders in construction or something. I can do that. I also want to eat like boJulius Malema."

I was tempted to judge him. To tell him that he was selling his soul. I could not see this mentality of his as sustainable. I knew it would kill something inside him. But maybe I should allow him to learn his own lessons.

It was clear that he was not your average gigolo. His intentions with these women were not to hurt them, but to get a small piece of their pie. It was a difficult time for men in South Africa. Affirmative action was not making it easier for them. Government and even the corporate sector were hiring and investing in women. Men were getting fewer opportunities; hence, some of them charmed women and used them to access opportunities. I read in a women's magazine that men who used women in this way were called "femigators."

"But tell me, are these powerful women that you are dating now connecting you to any tenders?" I asked.

"Not yet. It's in the pipeline. But you know most of them make my life easier in one way or another," he said.

"You know most people say that about their mothers. But then I guess you are not most people. Do you really think your life would be that difficult without them?" I asked.

My face might have said more than my words, because he kept quiet for a while and then replied, "You don't know anything about being poor. I can see you are from a middle-class family. All your siblings and parents are independent and affluent."

He rattled on: "You don't have a clue about how it is to struggle. You think you know this life. I look after myself and everyone in my family. I am the one who pays for my siblings' school and university fees. I am not only the source of bread but also the source of the table we put the bread on. You would never know what it's like. You see, I can't date young girls. You know how they are these days. They want money and they want to go out on dates. Everything is money, money, and I can't afford it. If I take that route, I won't be able to maintain my family. I could never be happy if my family is starving."

"Well, not all young girls are like that, some are very under-standing," I said.

"Not those that I attract."

"Maybe you attract those ones because you think all young girls are like that."

His cellphone rang and his face lit up. It was the Volvo lady. He did not even ask why she had been ignoring his calls.

"Hello, my love. Thank you for phoning. I miss you so much. I am sitting here alone and bored," he said, as if I were invisible. There was a pause before he said, "I don't have money for petrol, otherwise you know I would come to you now."

I reflected on the issues we had discussed. I wondered if he was using these women or if they were using him. My friend Ntombi said that successful women had evolved; they were cleverer than in the past. She said it used to be easy for gigolos to rob them of their hard-earned money. But these days women did not wish to empower the poor men. Although they promised them opportunities and tenders, they disposed of them like torn pantyhose when they found someone more appealing. I hoped it wasn't like that for Vusi.

I regarded him as a good neighbor, even though he never took out the garbage on Thursdays. I took his out along with mine because I hated the smell. Otherwise he never really bothered me. I shared my supper with him on days when I cooked a decent meal. When I had friends visiting, he would always bring us a bottle of champagne. It turned out that my friends were not his type. They were not full packages, or they were also looking for full packages. He tried approaching a few of them but never got lucky. Maybe it was because I had told them about him and his power houses.

After two weeks, my car was repaired. At times, I avoided him because I thought he was not stimulating enough for me. He hardly ever talked about his work. On days when I did not want to talk about affairs and relationship stuff, I smiled and greeted him and acted very busy and preoccupied. With time, he could tell when I was not in a chatty mood. As for him, he was never moody or offensive.

On one cold June night around midnight, I heard scratching noises at my door. It scared me and I called him on his cellphone. He phoned the security company. When the Hi-Tec Security guards arrived, we both went outside only to discover that it was a small dog. We did not know whose it was. I would have to take it to the vet the next morning. After the security officials left, we remained standing outside. It was two in the morning. He was alone that night, no girlfriend.

"How do you cope with this cold without a boyfriend?" he said. It was one of those days when I did not want to talk.

"I have a heater and an electrical blanket. They are warmer than any boyfriend," I said, closing the burglary door.

"No, man! You need a boyfriend, a real human heater. You need to have someone. When is your boyfriend coming? He probably has a roll-on too, a human blanket for winter," he insisted, looking at me through the door.

"Listen, I am fine, I am not a baboon. You know baboons like sex. They do it daily, exchanging partners. They can have sex the whole day because they don't have to be productive. Their food grows on trees. Some people are like baboons, all they do is have sex, as if one day they will fill a tank with it or receive an award for doing it often. All they think about is sex, sex, sex, all the time. Damn sex!"

By the time I had finished my tirade, he was in his cottage. I felt bad for being so harsh, but he had provoked me. He made me feel as if the fact that I was not having sex every day was a failing, or meant that I was abnormal. For some time, there were no more full-package conversations. Even his women-traffic slowed down a little. The Alfa Romeo lady became a regular.

I thought I had wished Vusi and his ways away, until one rainy Thursday night two weeks later. It was during the National Arts Festival. The small monumental town beamed with thousands of arty patriots come to take part in the festivities. I came home at about eleven in the evening after attending a show performed by my homeboy, the jazz artist Selaelo Selota.

I unlocked the main gate and then the smaller gate that led to our cottages. My cellphone rang as I was battling with the old rusty padlock.

"Hello, Makhi. Is it you opening the gate?" It was Vusi.

"Yes."

"Can you please come inside? I want to tell you something."

This was strange. We had been neighbors for five months and I had never been into his place.

Inside, he offered me beer.

After I'd had one, I asked, "What is it that you wanted to tell me?"

"I wanted to ask you to sleep in here tonight," he said, in the tone that one might use to ask to borrow a pen.

"What?"

"No, don't get me wrong. I just need company. We won't do anything. I just feel a little bit lonely tonight" he said, sounding like a young boy asking to sleep with his parents.

I laughed at him. "What is wrong? Can't you sleep alone?"

"I swear, we won't do anything," he pleaded. I noticed then that he was a bit intoxicated. In the bin next to the fridge were two bottles of wine.

"The last time someone pulled that trick on me, it was twenty-two years ago, when I was nineteen. Why don't you call one of your women to come and sleep with you?" I said, heading for the door.

"You know, I had my doubts, but now I am convinced that you are a borderline case."

I grabbed one more beer from the table and walked out. I was not angry, though. The whole thing was a joke. Even though I could never sleep with him, I was flattered by the fact that he found me attractive enough to try to persuade me. He was about fifteen years my junior and very handsome. *I've still got it*, I said to myself. I did not want to entertain the reality—that he was so messed up, he would be attracted to anything in a skirt.

Well, as I lay there on my bed, I could not help but fantasize about how it would have been. My mind was playing tricks on me. I really did not want to think such thoughts. It was crazy. If I had not understood the meaning of the word self-respect, I could have pursued him as an adventure—the same way his full packages must have done. *But I would hate myself*, I thought.

The following day he was so embarrassed that he could not even look me in the eye. When I locked the main gate before heading for the university, a short man with a curry complexion and a hanging stomach approached me. He got out of a Volkswagen Jetta. I had seen that car several times parked on the street adjacent to the next-door yard.

"Hello *sesi*," said the man sternly.

"Hello," I said. Although a bit tense, his eyes were too soft for him to be a thug.

"Can I ask you something? I won't take much of your time," he said in a deep Xhosa accent.

He asked me who lived in the house next to mine. He also asked me about a woman called Thembi, whom I said I didn't know. It was only when he mentioned the charcoal Alfa Romeo that I realized who he was talking about. Nevertheless, I decided to stick to my story—that I did not know her and I was really not good with cars, and would not know if I had seen a charcoal Alfa Romeo. I was embarrassed when the man said, "How can you not know an Alfa Romeo when you are driving one?"

"*Eish!* I am late for an appointment with my supervisor," I said, and disappeared into my car.

My day was so busy that I forgot all about this incident till later that evening, when I heard the sound of a breaking window. I peeped outside and saw two men holding Vusi and a third one striking his Corsa van with a wheel spanner. I quickly ran outside. When I reached them, the two men were still holding Vusi, but now the third one, the man with the curry complexion, was hitting him with the wheel spanner. Vusi moaned like a baby. It was like I was watching *The Godfather*. For once I wished we were living in the township. Help would have come instantly. Here in the suburbs, no one came out. I was the only spectator.

"Makhi, these people are going to kill me," Vusi cried when he saw me.

"This thing sleeps with my wife," the curry-complexioned man shouted. "Do you know how much *lobola* I paid for her? You think you can just have her for free? I'm going to kill this dog," he said, taking out a small gun from the inside pocket of his jacket.

I moved towards him and pleaded, "Sir! Please! Please! He

is just a careless boy. Please, papa, he has learned his lesson. Please! I beg you, don't mess your life up because of him! He has learned. He won't do it again. I beg you. Please!" I knelt between him and Vusi.

He paused and looked at me.

"Please, papa! Forgive him! He did not know what he was doing," I said with tears streaming from my eyes. I was not Vusi's biggest fan, but I did not want to see him murdered.

"She did not tell me that she was married. I did not know. I am sorry," Vusi said in his humblest voice.

"*Voetsek!* Keep quiet, you fucking fool," said the husband, while one of the other men kicked Vusi in the side.

"You must thank this woman. Otherwise I would have castrated you and burnt your testicles in your face. If you want to stay alive, keep away from my woman. Let's go," he said. The other two men threw Vusi on the Yesterday-today-tomorrow bush that was next to the gate.

"I am calling the police," I said, helping him out of the shrub.

"No! No police. *Eish!* I think he broke my knee with that wheel spanner," said Vusi.

He could not walk. "You will have to take me to the hospital," he said.

I phoned my classmate Charles to come and help me carry him. His car was smashed. When I saw Vusi at the hospital, under the bright lights, I could hardly recognize his face, it was now so swollen. I discovered that the PE lady's husband, having suspected his wife was having an affair, had trailed her movements for some time. Vusi stayed in hospital for three days. On his return, he moved out from the garden cottage and rented a small house in the township.

Our friendship faded after that. I bumped into him a few times in supermarkets but other than that, I did not know what he was doing. A year after the incident, he sent me an email announcing that he was getting married to the loud girl from the township. He asked me to give a speech at his wedding.

Glossary

A

a e tle ka disiti: money must be collected seat by seat

a go berekegi ka dikobong: he can't perform in bed

B

babelas: hangover

bogadi: in-laws' home

bona: look

buti: brother

C

chakalaka: spicy salad

D

dikgwatla: cow feet

donner: beat

E

Eish: used to express annoyance, surprise, or pain

G

gabotse botse: clearly

go padile: it's hopeless

goring? How are you?

I

inyanga: traditional healer/doctor

K

ke mathata: it's a problem

ke mehlolo: literally, the phrase means "These are miracles" but in this context, it means "This is crazy."

khethile: when you have made a choice and you can't change it

khotsi a Tshiandze: father of Tshiandze

khotsimuhulu: uncle

koko: grandmother

L

lefetwa: spinster

lekgowa: white person

lekwerekwere: foreigner

lobola: bride price

M

magogo: old lady

magolistos: 750 ml beer bottles

makhelwani: neighbor

makoti: daughter-in-law

mala: chicken intestines

malome: uncle

mamela: listen

mazwale: daughter-in-law

meerkat: mammal belonging to the mongoose family

mma: mother

modjadji: a rural girl (slang)

mogodu: cow or sheep stomach

mokgonyana: son-in-law

mokhaba: potbelly or big stomach

Mokokoroshi: Cornish-like chickens

mos: indeed

moroho: cooked pumpkin leaves

mutuku: sour porridge

mxe: a click made with the mouth that expresses distaste for something

N

ndaah: hello

ngwana mma: my sister

ngwanaka: my child

ntepa: traditional underwear with only a string at the back

nxa: a click made with the mouth that expresses extreme anger over something or someone

nyatsi: girlfriend of a married man

P

padkos: food for a journey

pap: maize porridge

plaasjapie: rural person

R

rondawels: thatched huts

S

sesi: sister

Shebeen: an unlicensed establishment or private house selling alcoholic liquor and typically regarded as slightly disreputable.

skheberesh: loose woman

sjambok: heavy leather whip

straatmeisie: a prostitute or ill-mannered, loose girl (slang)

T

theetsa: listen

tickiline: loose, undisciplined girl

tini: sour porridge

tshotsho: kickback

U

unjani wena? What kind of person are you?

uphilile? How are you?

V

voetsek: bug off, get lost

W

wena: you

wena ke wena o mobotse: you are beautiful

Y

yaa neh: an exclamation signifying agreement, yes, no

yoo nna mmawe: an exclamation that expresses being frightened and sometimes shock and dismay. Literally, it means calling one's mom. *Mmawe* is mom, *nna* is me

yoo: an exclamation which may express shock, pain, or being surprised

Acknowledgments

I want to thank the following people without whom I would not have had the courage to write and complete this book—my maternal grandparents, the late Stephen and Magdeline Muthivhi, who loved me more than anyone will ever be able to. My son Mohale Malatji, the sweetest young man. My brother Tebogo Malatji, the eternal optimist who always believes in me. He is my rock. My mother and father, John and Conny Malatji, who did their best to raise me well. My sisters Kgaugelo Malatji and Tumiso Mamasela for their undying support. My aunt Stella Muthivhi for being my shoulder.

All my teachers at Rhodes University, Robert Berold, Professor Laurence Wright, Professor Guy Berger and Hazel Crampton, Paul Wessels just to name a few.

My friends, Ivy Nkadimeng, Mpho Ledwaba, Mpho Phele, Molatelo Ramothwala, Ruth Woustra, Liz Gowen, Sabata Mafani, thank you for being the air beneath my wings.

To Enock Shibambo my soul provider.

Oceans of gratitude to those who assisted me in editing and coaching. Allessandre Condoti, Paul Mason and Bronwyn MacLennan.

And my utmost gratitude to Colleen Higgs of Modjaji books, who made being published a walk in the park for me.

And many, many thanks to those who made an effort to read my work and showered me with encouragement.

May they all be blessed with more than they dream of. Keleboga go menagane.

Lastly my praises goes to the Almighty who answered my prayers, making a dream real. If you have faith and hope you will have it all.

Discussion Questions

LOVE

1 The female characters in Malatji's stories—whether they remain single, get married, or have boyfriends—struggle to find committed romantic partners.

What are the obstacles standing in their way?

What are the cultural realities that make it difficult?

2 For the characters who find romantic love, what are their expectations for the relationship?

How well do those expectations match reality?

What expectations do the male characters have for their romantic female characters?

What conflicts do those expectations engender?

3 One of the realities that most of these characters face are romantic partners or spouses who cheat. This is sometimes explained away as "African culture."

What are your reactions to the women's experiences with their unfaithful partners and in particular to the idea that this is part of "African culture"?

Based on the variety of reactions and actions from characters in these stories, what do you suppose are Malatji's thoughts on the idea that this is a traditional part of their culture that women should just accept?

4 How does the romantic love experienced by these characters differ from your own experiences or desires/expectations?

What are you willing to accept in a relationship and what is a deal breaker for you?

FILIAL DUTY

1 The title story in this collection, "*Love Interrupted*," lays out the duties and responsibilities of the "*makoti*," or "daughter-in-law."

What are those duties and responsibilities?

This story offers a destructive example of how that can play out.

What are some of the problems the main character experiences and why?

How might these duties and responsibilities precipitate a mutually beneficial relationship between daughter-in-law and mother-in-law if both parties are kind and well-intended?

2 What are the responsibilities that adult children have towards their parents in this African culture?

How does that differ and how is it similar to those responsibilities that adult children have towards their parents in western culture?

PARENTHOOD

1 In many of these stories, women end up raising their children alone, even if they are married.

Why do you think that is so?

What are cultural, historical, and personal reasons that this happens?

2 What are the expectations for parenting in South Africa?

What is your definition of a "good mom"?

How do the characters in this book fulfill or fail your definition of "good mother"?

SOUTH AFRICA

1 What do you know about South Africa, either its current reality or its history?

2 How do these stories inform or shape your understanding of South African culture and history?

Did these stories confirm your expectations and understandings or provide new ways of looking at this country on the African continent?

3 Trace the theme of race and cross-cultural contact in *Love Interrupted*. When does connection occur and why?

When does disconnection or dissonance occur and why?

Does this collection offer you hope that South Africa can emerge from its racist past? Why or why not?

4 South Africa is often cited as a country with the highest differentials in income between the poor and the wealthy.

What accounts for the strong differences in income levels?

In this story, we have characters from all classes—from Lebo, who emerges from poverty to become a "black diamond," to characters who achieve a kind of cultural middle-class perspective if not wealth through education.

How do wealth and poverty shape the lives of the characters in these stories?

How do these factors shape the lives of people in western societies like the U.S.?

How do wealth and poverty shape the lives of people who lives in western nations, such as the U.S.?

What are the differences and what are the similarities?

OTHER BOOKS FROM CATALYST PRESS

Dark Traces, *by Martin Steyn*

The body of a teenage girl is found in the veld near an upper middle-class suburb of Cape Town, South Africa. The pathologist remembers a similar case. The last thing recently widowed Detective Jan Magson feels like taking on is a serial killer file, but alongside Inspector Colin Menck, he follows the trail. And every time a lead reaches a dead end, Magson finds himself looking down at another dead girl, wondering how he's going to make it through the dark traces of yet another night, alone, a service pistol at his side.

Sacrificed, *by Chanette Paul*

Rejected by her parents, sister, husband, everyone except her extraordinary daughter, Caz Colijn lives a secluded life in her own little patch of Africa. But a single phone call from her estranged sister shatters her refuge. From the Congo's sparkling diamond mines to Belgium's finest art galleries, from Africa's civil unrest to its deeply spiritual roots, *Sacrificed* seamlessly crosses borders and decades with a fiercely captivating story.

We Kiss Them With Rain, *by Futhi Ntshingila*

Life wasn't always hard for fourteen-year-old Mvelo. But now her mother is dying of AIDS and what happened to Mvelo remains unspoken, despite its growing presence. *We Kiss Them With Rain* explores both humor and tragedy in this modern-day fairytale set in a squatter camp outside of Durban, South Africa, in which the things that seem to be are only a façade and the things that are revealed and unveiled create a happier, thoroughly believable, alternative.

The Lion's Binding Oath and Other Stories, *by Ahmed Ismail Yusuf*

Through stories that span the years before and during Somalia's civil war, Ahmed Ismail Yusuf weaves together Somalia's political, social, and religious conflicts with portrayals of the country's love of poetry, music, and soccer. Yusuf's collection is a powerful examination of love and resilience in a country torn apart by war and written with deep compassion for the lives of its characters.

BOOKS BY STORY PRESS AFRICA, an imprint of Catalyst Press

Shaka Rising: A Legend of the Warrior Prince
a graphic novel by Luke Molver

A charismatic young warrior prince emerges from exile to usurp the old order and forge a new, mighty Zulu kingdom. This retelling of the Shaka legend explores the rise to power of a shrewd young prince who must consolidate a new kingdom through warfare, mediation, and political alliances to defend his people against the expanding slave trade.